C. Tauske 1/ '01
P. Lieberman 2/ '01

THE SIN EATER

BY

ALICE THOMAS ELLIS

IN COMMON READER EDITIONS:

The Sin Eater
The Birds of the Air
The 27th Kingdom
The Other Side of the Fire
Unexplained Laughter
The Clothes in the Wardrobe
The Skeleton in the Cupboard
The Fly in the Ointment
The Inn at the Edge of the World
Pillars of Gold
The Evening of Adam
Fairy Tale
A Welsh Childhood
Home Life Volumes One — Four

ALSO BY ALICE THOMAS ELLIS:
Wales: An Anthology (edited with Kyffin Williams)
Serpent on the Rock: A Personal View of Christianity
Cat Among the Pigeons
WITH TOM PITT-AIKENS:
Secrets of Strangers
The Loss of the Good Authority

THE SIN EATER

Alice Thomas Ellis

A COMMON READER EDITION
THE AKADINE PRESS

The Sin Eater

A COMMON READER EDITION published 1998
by The Akadine Press, Inc., by arrangement with the author.

A COMMON READER EDITION and fountain colophon
are trademarks of The Akadine Press, Inc.

ISBN 1-888173-36-X

3   5   7   9   10   8   6   4   2

TO JOSH

'GOODBYE,' SAID ROSE. 'Remember – please and thank you, no strangers, and don't fall in the lake.'

'Oh Mum,' said the twins, laughing. They both leaned out of the car window, their faces damp from washing, their hair sleek as water in the sun. 'Oh Mum.'

Rose laughed too. They were such competent, beautiful little children, not the sort to come to harm.

'Don't you worry, Mrs Ellis,' yelled Jack, grinding the gears.

'Slowly up the pass,' she cried, unheard, as the car backed noisily out of the double gateway into the lane. Jack the Liar had had several small mishaps recently – he would bring the car back dented and bruised, long trails of leaves and hedge-grass and sinister tufts of virgin sheep's wool clinging to the door handles. 'Bloody maniacs on the road,' he'd say, stepping about unsteadily. But he was sober now. Rose had smelt his breath and discerned only a chronic and lingering halitosis.

It was the drinking season: seductive holiday weather when even the locals still at work drank too much at lunchtime and early in the evening. The cold respectable grip of the chapels had lost its power, and people drank as they had drunk all those years before when the bay was dry land and the prince had built his castle there among the flowering cornfields and the woods alive with game.

7

Then the sea had been almost out of sight beyond the horizon where now a boat was appearing, crawling into view like a cockroach over a rope. Centuries had passed since the servant had run into the great hall crying to the prince that the fishes were swimming in the cellars and the prince had poured himself another drink. His daughter, who disapproved of him, had led the survivors up here to watch as the sea washed over their fields and their farms. That was the legend. Certainly the country had been much subject to inundation and there were other bays and lakes where church bells rang from the depths and the lean remains of dwellings could be seen below when the water was still and clear. These days holiday makers swam and frolicked and floated about in the bay, fathoms above the sunken castle and the drowned, drunken courtiers. 'Let them drink their fill,' the princess had remarked as the tide rose. It sounded worse in Welsh.

The eminence where the *Plâs* was built had since been known by a name which could mean either Weeping or Watching Point. It was probable that the princess had watched and the dispossessed peasants had wept, since the mountain slopes offered nothing like the living they had known on the disappearing plain with its fair broad fields and placid river. Only the princess had preferred the wind-swept heights, being of a harsh and austere temperament. She had left her father's surviving subjects to manage as best they could and climbed even higher in search of the lonely sanctity she had always craved. Now Rose requested her to keep an eye open for the twins who would pass within a few miles of her abandoned hermitage. Civilly, Rose added 'Amen'.

The momentary chill of parting was indistinguishable from the wind that came up from the sea even on the best days. Rose disregarded it. Some gnats were dancing over the rain butt, like a veil being violently shaken. The twins danced sometimes – unselfconsciously and fast. They lifted their knees high, dipped their heads, spread their arms . . .

It was very quiet. Rose could hear the spiders who lived in the ivy rustling discontentedly. A single butterfly hung, drained, on a dusty web. Spiders knew nothing of sumptuary laws, but Jack had been spraying the garden with insecticide again. It was his favourite gardening task: simple, unstrenuous and with such satisfactorily immediate results.

His mother appeared at the kitchen door, for no other purpose than to convey displeasure. She stood quite still, her hands at her sides, looking grim. Her lips were as hard, as bitterly thin, as split slate, and her eyes were small and black and dull. She was dressed, unconventionally for the sick-room, in a flowered overall and gumboots.

'They've gone,' said Rose in the empty yard.

Phyllis said nothing. Rose was meant to guess what had upset her and offer amends, even an apology. It was quite possible that if she went towards the kitchen Phyllis would refuse to give way and they would stand there nose to nose like cats for an incalculable time. Instead, she turned and began to walk round the stable yard, and when she looked back Phyllis had disappeared: she would be making something special for Gomer's tea, something luscious and greasy with butter and sultanas, to spite her employers and make her grandson happy and fatter.

Rose began to miss the twins. She touched the bark of

the sycamore and told herself they would have a lovely time staying with the Captain's old cousins. They could play by the lake with the pretty, useless animals – Jacob's sheep and Japanese pheasants – and eat wild wormy raspberries and the little brown trout from the streams. Rose anticipated for them, against all probability and experience, hours of mild water and unflawed sunshine. It was good for them to be away for a time. Death was waiting in the house like a bailiff, quiet and unobtrusive but not fit company for the children, who were too young to learn the nature of intransigence.

'How's the Captain?' she asked, stopping and leaning in through the open kitchen window.

'The Captain's fine,' said Phyllis loudly to the table, on which she was stamping out little rounds of pastry. She was not so disgruntled as to ignore a direct question.

'The twins will be back next week,' offered Rose, quite aware that it was not the twins' welfare that concerned Phyllis.

Surprise briefly lightened Phyllis's expression of resentment. She closed her mouth tightly and stamped out more little rounds with the controlled rhythmic rage of marching feet. She didn't look up. She was riddled through with anger and depression.

Rose continued her perambulation. The slate flags, recently hosed down, gleamed, and the pools of dampness under the hydrangeas reflected impossible depths. The mountain beyond was misty in the heat and the lichen on the stone wall crackled drily under her hand. She wore a long blue dress and looked like an angel between the sky and the purple ground. Her hair was cut close to her skull, as black as the bird admonishing her, staccato, from the sycamore, and her eyes were huge and round and blue like windows, cut not to see through, but to show the sky.

*   *   *

Michael and Angela had been driving for hours. The car was hot, untidy with bits of paper and bad temper. They went slowly through the twisting streets of an old walled town planned, successfully, for the repulsion and impediment of non-residents.

'If we go this way we'll come out on the pass,' said Angela.

Michael just prevented himself from running over a small child clad in pants and bra and eating sweets under the overhang of an Elizabethan house.

'Careful,' said Angela.

'The coast road,' said Michael, enunciating clearly, 'will be solid with traffic.'

'You don't *know* that,' said Angela.

They'd been quarrelling covertly for a long time now, to the danger of other motorists. Angela had a large repertory of small sounds, not usually associated with aggression. She would sniff, cough, tap her fingers, hum quietly on clear stretches of road. Michael used the car to startle and alarm, speeding round corners, overtaking lorries. Neither of them was given to open displays of anger. They came from the same background – conventional, incurious, outwardly pacific. But confined spaces and solitude didn't suit them. Without other people and distraction they regressed and bickered in a sexless, pre-pubertal way.

'There's a caravan in front,' observed Angela. It

trundled ponderously along, taking up a lot of road. Michael moved to the right. Instantly, out of nowhere, they were faced by a station-wagon crammed with an extended family and what must have been a large proportion of its worldly possessions. Michael moved back behind the caravan, but not before a great deal of terror and bad feeling had been engendered in the three vehicles.

'The most dangerous road in the whole of Wales and you start driving like a madman,' cried Angela, forced by fright into the open.

'Oh, rubbish,' said Michael, shaken. 'I've been driving up and down here since I was ten.'

Angela snorted.

The pass wound like a broken spring down the mountainside. On the left the gaunt rockface thrust out pugnaciously, not giving an inch, and on the right the mountain fell sheerly away in a great waste of stone and shale to a dry river bed. Two houses stood at the bottom looking defenceless and foolish like bystanders caught uncomprehending between opposing factions. Angela was too annoyed to remark that she wouldn't like to live down there. But the pass was levelling out. Suddenly it became nothing worse than a country road bordered by hedges that broke here and there to show the sea shining beyond the fields. They went through a hamlet scarcely visible behind cigarette ads, an inn sign, banners heralding ice-cream and boards announcing *Gwely a Brecwast* and Fish and Chips. One smugly offered home-made scones. Parking, said the signs. Ladies, Inn Food, No Parking, Coca Cola, No Entrance, *Dim Parcio*, Conveniences, Campers Welcome, No Dogs, Fairy Glen, *Ar Werth*, For Sale, No Overnight Parking, *Merched,*

Women, *Cyfleusterau*, Gents. A local girl was pushing a pram. Visitors drank pints and idled over the little bridge. Nervous Welsh sheep dogs minced girlishly along the roadside, each rolling one blind milk-blue eye. On the left a sign, slightly askew, welcomed all comers. *Croeso Llanelys*, it said.

Angela sat up, pulled at her skirt and patted her cheeks with a paper handkerchief. Michael turned the car abruptly up a steep mountain lane, changed down twice and drove into the stable yard of his father's house. He turned off the engine and got out.

*　　*　　*

Rose came forward and opened the door for her sister-in-law. People being helped out of cars were always at a disadvantage. 'A new car,' she remarked. 'What a pretty colour.'

'It's awfully hot,' said Angela accusingly, getting out stiffly and looking around.

'You look hot,' agreed Rose, standing back so that there could be no question of kissing – the smell of other people's hair and teeth. She was gratified to see they both wore silly hats.

Angela took hers off. It was in the Spanish mode – broad-brimmed, shallow-crowned and an emphatic shade of orange. She shook her hair, which was fair and dressed in large waves high off her forehead like a lady parliamentarian's: feminine, but reliable, with the merest hint of intellect. She looked disconsolate – odd against the lovely day.

'How's Father?' asked Michael from the boot of the car,

13

where he was pulling out suitcases and bags. His blue denim cap – the type worn by foreign workmen and ageing literary agents – shaded his eyes and hid his expression.

'He's just the same,' said Rose, though the same as what, she didn't say. He certainly was not as he had been.

Phyllis was back in the kitchen doorway. 'Angela, Michael,' she said, a bit grudgingly but politely enough.

'Phyllis,' cried Angela. 'How *are* you? And Jack and Gomer?'

'Oh, we're well,' said Phyllis, even smiling a little now, though not so much in response to Angela as at the mention of her grandson.

'I think you're marvellous,' said Angela, ' – taking on nursing the Captain as well as looking after this great big house.'

'We manage,' said Phyllis unblushingly. She stumped off to what Jack called the kitchen garden: a small stony patch behind the hydrangeas containing some wilting beans and a few lettuces. Rose got all her vegetables from a market-garden up the valley – they were fresh and brittle and professionally symmetrical – but Jack made great play with his little plot, tossing around spadefuls of earth in the early evening if anyone happened to be watching, and triumphantly flinging down yellowing cabbages on the kitchen table. 'How's that then?' he'd say. 'Terrific,' Rose would answer, eyes averted.

Phyllis stepped back out of the hydrangeas carrying a sprig of mint before her.

'Roast lamb, eh?' called Michael cheerily. 'I say, Phyllis, where's that lazy great Gomer? He can take these

14

up.' He indicated the suitcases and smiled expectantly.

Phyllis simply behaved as though he had not spoken. She walked straight past them into the house and quietly closed the door which, all through the summer, stood open until sunset. Michael stared after her.

'She's mad,' said Rose consolingly.

Michael turned his face away in irritation. He didn't need Rose to explain his father's servants to him. And anyway servants were often comic, and occasionally eccentric, but they weren't mad.

'Phyllis is one of the sanest people I know,' said Angela; 'and underneath that reserve she's terribly pleased to see us. She's always had such a soft spot for Michael.'

But Rose had seen Phyllis's face, sullen and set with bitterness, contrasting strangely with the delicate faceted globes of hydrangea.

'She's probably feeling desperately overworked,' said Angela. 'It must be a frightful strain looking after the Captain as well as everything else.'

'She doesn't do anything else,' said Rose. 'A woman comes to do the rough and I do the cooking.'

Angela never believed Rose. 'She still has Jack and Gomer to look after and her own house,' she said rebukingly.

'They all spend their time here,' said Rose. 'They like it much better.'

'Well, if Father can't be moved, you should have a properly trained nurse,' said Angela. 'I shall speak to Henry about it as soon as he gets here.'

Rose didn't want a trained nurse, but she said nothing. There was plenty of time. 'When Ermyn comes,' she promised, 'Phyllis will take you all to see your father.'

15

'Ah yes,' said Michael nervously. He picked up a pea-stick and beat it against his leg. 'I think I'll just have a look round.'

Angela smiled after him to show Rose how tenderly good wives treated their husbands. 'He always does that,' she said, determinedly fond. 'Goes to make sure everything's just the same – like a little boy.'

'Or a dog,' said Rose. 'Dogs do that too.'

'You would know more about that than I,' said Angela distinctly, intending to wound. Rose's father had been the local vet – though no one believed he had actually qualified. He had been Irish and disreputable, and she could never understand why Rose didn't mind. 'I think I'll go after Michael,' she said.

*   *   *

Rose sat down on the slate slab that ran the length of the old dairy at right angles to the house. The stables had been partly demolished when the Captain sold his horse, and the sun, unhindered, filled the yard. The ivy that grew on the mortarless stone walls was so thick Rose could sit in its shade. It had fleshless sinewy branches like the arms of the old men who had been sheep farmers in the hills not so long before. Now the native population was entirely dedicated to fleecing tourists – not such a healthy life, but easier. Every house with as much as one spare bedroom or parlour was given up to this seasonal occupation, and avarice could have been shown on the map as a border running round the coastline and reappearing inland wherever a natural lake, a significant waterfall or a pleasant stretch of countryside was likely to attract

16

the tourist trade. 'The Principality is tantamount to a catamite,' said Rose.

Occasionally she could hear, very faintly, the sound of footsteps and voices on the other side of the high stone wall – visitors going to have a look at the standing stones of the Druids' circle and the refreshment kiosk that stood nearby in case anyone should sink from famine three miles from civilisation.

She fetched a basket of peas and an earthenware bowl from the larder and sat down again. She had meticulously planned all the meals for the next few days and every detail was clear in her mind. She had never been one for the lovable muddle or the endearing smudge of flour on the cheek. She was greedy and clever and cynical, qualities essential to a good cook, and sometimes she used her ingredients like a witch, as social comment, to do mischief, or as a benefice. When Angela came back she would be met by the exasperating sight of Rose performing a domestic task carefully and well, and looking cool.

'I can't find him,' complained Angela, wandering round the side of the house. 'He's gone too far.' She sat down and plucked a large ivy leaf to fan herself. 'It's so *hot*,' she said. 'Shall I do those for you?'

'I've done them,' said Rose putting the peas aside. 'I think I might show you your room now.'

Angela was puzzled but, as yet, unsuspicious. 'I *know* our room,' she said. 'We always have it.'

'It's different,' said Rose. 'I've changed it a bit.' She spoke carefully, not wanting to spoil her effect.

They went in through the kitchen door. The slate flags continued all over the ground floor of the *Plâs* except for the drawing-room, the Captain's study and the room

17

known as the long parlour, where wide boards had been laid to alleviate the dampness in the days before central heating.

Angela noticed how well the house was looking. Its windows and wood shone with cleanliness, and it had the complacent, untroublesome air of a well-cared-for child. This was probably because Phyllis had more time now that Gomer was older.

'You could carpet these stairs you know, Rose,' Angela said, as her smart shoes cracked at the wooden staircase. 'It wouldn't detract at all from the feeling of the house.'

Rose stopped on the landing and opened a door. It was the same door, but the room within was quite different.

Angela stared, suddenly breathless. She looked quickly at Rose expecting to catch a wicked smile, but Rose's expression was as bland as the top of the milk.

'They did a lot to this part of the house at this period,' said Rose. 'I expect it was with all the money Henry's mother brought. It's always had a pre-war feeling, and I thought now was the time to make it explicit. Because,' she went on, 'no one really likes this style, and by the time they do it will be too late.'

Angela was speechless. She wanted to say that Rose had behaved unforgivably, that she had no right to change and distort things like this. She hated the room: the geometric furniture, the pale green carpet with the darker band, the embroidered antimacassars on the buff moquette armchair. All offended, not merely her taste, but her sense of caste.

'We must get you some flowers,' said Rose. 'Lupins, I think, or marigolds in a nice black pot.' Rather to her sur-

18

prise, she had grown to like the room. It had a comfortable afternoon air, ordered and respectable, redolent of a time when staid steady people had small families, dug in the allotment, listened to the wireless and drank cocoa before going to bed. Part of her fondness for the house was based on the ease with which she could make a fool of it, and she sometimes seemed to herself like one of those selfless persons who dedicate their lives to a poor amiable upper-class madman – putting his gloves on the wrong hands, setting his beret straight over his eyebrows, taking their time wiping soup off his chin. Never sadistic, just gently amused.

'What happened to the other furniture?' asked Angela. She didn't want to sound grasping and inquisitive, but she did want to know. The solid mahogany, the bevelled glass, the brass handles . . .?

Rose had considered saying that she had given it to a man who came with a cart, but the truth would do as well. 'It's in the attic,' she said. 'I could send it to London if you like.'

'I wouldn't dream of taking father's furniture away,' said Angela, annoyed by this offer of what, after all, she had as much right to as Rose. 'It's much too big for Albert Terrace.' She had just finished furnishing her new house in the style Rose described as 'solicitor's regency' – desks inlaid with gold-tooled leather, brocade curtains, crimson-striped wallpaper, velvet-wrapped chaises longues, tiny teetering pie-crust tables and little framed silhouettes cascading down the walls. Each room was now complete and nothing more would fit in.

'I think I've got it right,' said Rose, taking a final look round. 'It's a very pure and consistent style. They thought

19

about it a lot. It didn't just evolve.' She closed the door quietly.

Alone in the room Angela flung her handbag on to the folkweave counterpane of the chubby bed. Michael's home had always seemed an extension of her life, a rightful heritage, a reminder of the past where, previously, she had felt she was coming into her own. She felt almost overwhelmed by detestation of the interloper.

There was a large photograph in a tortoiseshell frame on the chest of drawers. It was a wedding picture. Now she came to think of it, there were a lot of photographs of Rose's wedding around the house – she was sure Rose scattered them out of pure spite. In this one Rose and Henry stood smiling at each other, surrounded by their respective families, who were not smiling at anyone and were clearly telling themselves that the whole thing was a dreadful mistake. *Henry*, thought Angela furiously. When she'd heard he was planning to marry the only daughter of a large Irish family who lived in the village she'd thought he must have gone mad. She'd envisaged bare mud-encrusted feet, green petticoats and safety-pinned shawls, bloodshot noses, building-site boots and perhaps the tell-tale outline of a small pig buttoned beneath the bright blue double-breasted suits. The reality had been worse. Rose's brothers were gentle, softly spoken young men in jobs that might one day make them rich; her father, although an obvious knave, succulent with confident charm, and her mother a stern respectable woman of the sort who would have made an excellent housekeeper or nanny in a more sensible age. And Rose was undeniably a good-looking girl, if you cared for that exaggerated style. None of them, not one, had admired

Angela – not her appearance, not her conversation, not her hat. They had been irreproachably polite, but their politeness had concealed the most hurtful of all insults: their ideals and aspirations were quite different from her own. It had been obvious that they considered Rose to be throwing herself away on Henry and it was a sorry waste – a view of the situation so novel that Angela had then too found herself at a loss for words. They had stood together looking a little critical and disappointed. Only when they had caught sight of Rose in her great lacy wedding gown had their faces relaxed and broken into the kind of reassured smile that had obviously been used before and was kept for Rose. Rose had shared their mirth, trailing her train insolently like the tail of her coat, her wreath of small yellow roses slipping over one eye. It was as though a practical joke was in process. Angela remembered vividly the mild indecorousness of the occasion – not the usual nuptial jollity, but an oddly irreverent atmosphere, light and ungrateful. She had put it down at the time to Roman Catholicism.

*   *   *

Ermyn was still on the train – gathered into the corner, legs tightly crossed, her cheek stuck damply to her palm, trying to tidy up her mind. It was difficult, because the journey was distracting. The train hurried along so purposefully on lines all laid out for it, stretching as far as it needed to go – like a crown prince or a bride. Her own future was shadowy and obstacle-ridden and she had no clear picture even of the present. It seemed foolish to envy a train, but its determination was astounding, as it clung to the rails, slicing through the countryside with

21

such speed, such pertinacity. Ermyn's mind wandered incorrigibly. She watched her fellow passengers furtively, puzzled. They moved about a great deal, closing windows, pushing at doors, buying things to eat and drink, and seemed enviably calm – not high-spirited precisely, but free from anxiety. They spoke little except to offer one another crisps and chocolate, threaten their children or speculate briefly about the temporary disposition of the cat they had left behind. How could they bear themselves, she wondered guiltily – so shapeless and plain? How could they marry each other – how content themselves with such inferiority? Did they not realise there were some who would rather be dead than married to them? Perhaps it was just genetic, as with orang-outans or crocodiles – they kept themselves to themselves and seemed not to mind that other creatures found them undesirable. Or take the music master at school. It was said that several times each term girls would wake screaming and sobbing and, when questioned, confess they had dreamed they were standing before the altar beside the music master: yet he had a wife and she never complained. But their clothes, thought Ermyn, glancing sideways at the travellers – how could they wear them, brilliantly coloured and patterned, dazzlingly white, permanently pleated, synthetic, unventilated? She was uncomfortably hot in a loose cotton smock, but they seemed impervious to the atmosphere, zipped into layers of artificial cloth. They were alien: ugly prosperous Midlanders with an air of almost menacing mistrust. She realised, astonished, that they considered themselves as good as her any day, and her picture of the working classes wavered and faded. Wherever they were, those jolly, shirt-sleeved, fish-and-chip-eating, knees-up masses, they weren't on this train going for their holidays to the Welsh coast.

Two children stood across the aisle gazing, calf-like, at the incomprehensible stranger to whom they meant nothing. What if she were to offer them an apple? Their parents would seize it, examine it suspiciously, and throw it angrily away.

Ermyn turned her head and looked out of the window. Now she would think of Father, whose blood had reneged on him – on Father, who set such store by loyalty. All those individual corpuscles had abandoned their respectable solitariness and together rushed to the citadel to destroy the master, had formed into a group to undo him. She wondered whether, having struck its blow, the traitorous fluid had returned, satisfied, to its normal peaceful highways and byways, flowing quietly along. Father had always taken good care of his blood, had married it into one of the oldest families in England, had brought it home unspilt from the war, had dedicatedly taken a patent purifying powder whenever he felt a little liverish, had been careful to exclude from his shooting parties anyone whose birth and breeding might have made him a poor risk – in Father's view only very dubious people had accidents with guns – and all in all deserved better of it than it had rendered him. She, at least – a princess of his blood – would not turn against him, nor forget him. It would be wrong to let him go quite alone. If she could imagine the transition, the way out, it would make it less alarming for him. He might just catch a glimpse of her spirit on some unthinkable threshold and feel reassured.

Ermyn closed her eyes to practise dying and had an impression of discomfort, light, cold and a taste of salt. Surprised, she opened her eyes. That was not as she would have imagined. She had thought it would be darker and warmer, at least to begin with. Her fellow travellers had been nowhere important. They were still getting up and down, not talking, not reading their papers. They made no demands on her, expected nothing of her, except – when the time came for her to get off and disturb them – perhaps a perfect, almost religious politeness. Ermyn wished the journey would go on forever. Decisions and changes – even those so comparatively minor as getting off a train – distressed her. There was no one here to whom she need actively respond. It was a time out of time, like all journeys, and arrival would be too sudden, no matter how carefully she had prepared herself; her heart would start to thud, her hands to sweat. She told herself it would merely be a tiresome interruption, like being called away from a picture book. The countryside flipped by, brightly coloured and simplified by speed: green pages illuminated with cows and castles, canals and geese – there was no opportunity to dwell on detail. Reality, with all its unpleasing aspects, stood no chance at this pace.

The train sped round a bend. They went through a suburb resting in the sunlight, the backs of the houses innocently exposed and revealing. There was shining glass and grass everywhere: picture windows, green-houses, and smooth satisfied lawns; flowering shrubs and nice clean women preparing supper for their appreciative families. Sometimes through a gap she could see the façades of houses across the road, tightly closed and buttoned, expressionless, determined to repel curiosity

24

and even interest. It was out at the back that life went on – spilling into the long gardens, framed in the windows – and the people didn't know, or had forgotten, that the iron caterpillar rushing past contained intelligent, observing life. What a butterfly would emerge, should the train ever reach the chrysalis stage. What a vast metallic flapping as it took off, its wings stamped with an irregular collage of flattened passengers . . . Ermyn suspected that this thought was morbid and put it out of her mind.

The industrial towns had the appeal of fiction – unreal, evocative. The little factories looked complete and efficient. Ermyn imagined workers, contented after a day of fulfilling labour, preparing to go home to kippers and crumpets cooked over a glowing fire. Everything was reduced, silenced and sweetened by distance – the slum houses, back to back, cosy and neighbourly; the playing-fields the sites of friendly competition. Only as they got nearer to the sea, to territory that Ermyn knew and had visited, did her interest fail. Now she saw that every mile or so there stood red-brick or grey-stone buildings holed and ruined, and in their place were going up things made of pre-cast concrete and sheets of plastic. The neat settlements and orderly fields gave way to miles of caravan sites: occasional retreats, exploited and unloved, set out in rows like graveyards for the living. And the rubbish dumps piled with old cars no longer had the distant charm of abandoned nurseries.

Ermyn didn't want to go back. She was only just out of childhood, and time had not yet done its work on the past – breaking it down into something that would be acceptable, even fruitful. It still had the horrid immediacy of the dustbin, and her memories were recognisable and unpleasantly pungent.

She permitted herself to consider her idea. She'd had it for some time. It had begun as an impossible idea, extravagant, exotic and unmentionable. Now it was becoming less strange and a source of comfort, as precious, as promising of fulfilment, as a baby or a key. Father wouldn't like it. But then Father probably wouldn't be here much longer. Ermyn screwed up her eyes and gritted her teeth. What was wrong with her mind that thoughts could emerge in it unbidden by her will? Anyway, Father didn't seem to care about Rose being a Roman Catholic, so perhaps he wouldn't mind as much as she imagined. Ermyn's religious yearnings were the result not so much of an urge towards virtue as of a fear of evil and unkindness. The Church seemed to her a very good and powerful thing, combining as it did the qualities of rocks and lambs – and kings, she thought confusedly, and fish . . .

Quite suddenly the sea was there. It lay casually alongside the track, looking calm and indifferent, its boundaries obscured by the sun shining in her eyes. She looked up anxiously to see if her suitcase was still on the rack. Once through the tunnel and past the iron bridge that spanned Elys Water it would be time to go and stand by the door. The train stopped only briefly at Llanelys and soon, if the railway authorities had their way, it wouldn't stop at all. She edged out of her seat, begging the pardon of several people, carefully opened, and then closed, the compartment door, pulled the window down and slid her profile just barely into the sea-smelling air. When she was very young a man had had his head knocked clean off against

26

the iron bridge. Jack the Liar had been passing at the time, along the road that lay parallel to the railway. The head was right up Elys Water, he'd said, hoarse with the thrill – they were hours finding it.

The iron bridge swept by. Ermyn closed her eyes against the hateful edifice and Elys Water gibbering beneath it like a chained maniac. The breeze was strong and cool and she could hear the brief shouts of people running in and out of the sea. The train slowed and the shouts became louder, the breeze less. She could see the Ocean View Café and the bowling green with people walking on it and children licking ice-creams. Home at last, thought Ermyn wretchedly.

The train stopped short of the platform and she had to jump. But she was a big strong girl and managed better than the lady behind her, who had to lower herself backwards.

'Do let me help you,' said Ermyn, hindering rather, as the lady strove for a foothold.

'Here's my friend,' said the lady, relieved. She gave Ermyn a hostile look and moved away, talking intensely about the weather.

The platform was hot. Those of Ermyn's fellow passengers who had alighted with her walked off confidently towards the bored ticket collector. Perhaps they had never been here before, but they knew where they were going, walking without a moment's doubt in the right direction.

Ermyn stood by her suitcase, tasting the smell of ozone and melting tar, determined not to cry. Pink and white columbine and green blackberries were strung out along the platform's edge and bees buzzed among them. She began to walk, not having decided which road to take.

'I'll leave my case here,' she said to the ticket collector. 'Jack will pick it up later.'

'He'd better look smart,' said the man disrespectfully. 'I'm off at six.'

Outside the station she stopped again and glanced at an imaginary watch. Either road would take her through the village, with its one shopping street, and the old ladies of Llanelys would hail her, accost her – those harmless, false-toothed predators. But Ermyn felt boneless and vulnerable, unable to cope with them. They would dart out of nowhere like small stupidly inquisitive fish, crying, 'Well, Ermyn, do you remember me?' And she never did. They were all the same, undifferentiated. 'Terrible thing about your *da*,' they'd say; 'such a fine big man', watching her hungrily, avid for tears. She never understood why they were always in the village, washed, with their hats on. They never seemed to buy very much; yet they were always in the shops, heads together, sliding out sly Welsh words between their lips. And when she passed their houses they were always there too, sitting in pairs across tables set perfunctorily for tea, by the window behind the china dogs and the artificial tulips, eyes watchful, ears pricked.

She went up the hill very fast, smiling indiscriminately, surprising several visitors who had never seen her before.

*   *   *

Michael was in the drawing-room. It was cool and full of the blue sea light. The green-gold plush of a big wing-chair gleamed shallowly where it curved like the breasts

28

of small animals. Cool-cheeked roses creamed over the rim of a green bowl similarly painted with roses.

'This is a lovely room,' said Angela, walking in and relaxing as her confidence returned. She wondered whether to mention the bedroom but decided against it. Rose, though awful, was known to be clever, and it could well be that that frightful style was about to become fashionable. Michael could make what he liked of it for himself. She moved among the furniture remarking on this and that. She never felt quite right unless she was telling people things: she felt she owed it to herself to impress her personality on her surroundings and had discovered she could best do this by assertion. 'It's what I always call a *traditional* drawing-room.' The element of pastiche introduced by Rose – the tropical shells displayed on a small table, the wax flowers under a glass dome – seemed to have escaped her notice.

The tea-table was set in front of the west fireplace. There were two of these in the room – the other was on the north wall – and they were lit according to the direction of the prevailing wind. Immediately above the west fireplace the Captain's wife had caused a window to be set. It was customary in the family to complain about it. The Captain's wife, despite her undoubted breeding and wealth, had had artistic leanings, and although she had been dead for seventeen years the Captain still blamed her for draughts and occasional smoke from the contorted chimney.

Glass, silver and china glittered on a lace table-cloth, an unused wedding present to the Captain's wife that Rose had found in a trunk. Here too pastiche was evident, though not to Angela, who thought everything was as nice

29

as this despite Rose, who had expended considerable thought on the matter.

'Indian or China?' invited Rose. 'Milk or lemon?'

'These cups are new, aren't they?' asked Angela, examining one closely. It was pale blue and white and bore a design depicting an animal caught upside down in a thicket.

Rose agreed that they were new and explained that she had found them in a sale when she was looking for anti-macassars. She knew quite well that Angela was wondering what had happened to the Crown Derby; she wasn't going to tell her it was put safely away in the china pantry. She offered a plate of cucumber sandwiches – tiny, damp and neat. Angela gobbled up several, unaware of malice: they suited her style to perfection. There were scones sinking in butter in a covered dish and a madeira cake shot with cherries, an emerald bow of angelica on its bald and furrowed pate.

'You are lucky to have Phyllis,' she told Rose. 'I was awfully afraid when we moved that I wouldn't be able to find anyone. We thought at first they might resent us. You know . . .'

'I know,' said Rose. Michael and Angela had sold their Kensington house to finance one of Michael's business deals and had bought another in a district in North London that was 'coming up'. Their friends thought this dashing of them, although the street had been entirely taken over by designers, architects and TV producers (described by Rose as 'the new illiteracy' and known collectively as 'Albert Terrace Man'). Meanwhile the native population had moved to the less pleasant area behind the High Street, where the council had built flats for them at almost inconceivable expense. They nearly all disliked these flats, and their young had sprayed messages on the smooth featureless walls so admirably adapted to the purpose, in letters eight-feet high, expressing, to the best of their ability, their displeasure and resentment. They had broken all the external lighting and mugged each other in the lifts, car parks and darkened alleyways.

'Anyway,' Angela went on, 'the very first day we moved I went into the newsagents to put in a notice for a char, and the shop was full of the old things in their slippers and curlers and they couldn't have been nicer. My Mrs T. came to me at once and she hardly ever misses a day. She's marvellous with the children and they adore her.'

'You can always get someone if you're prepared to pay enough,' said Rose.

There was a rather pained silence.

'Oh no,' said Michael and Angela together.

'It isn't the money,' explained Angela. 'Phyllis wouldn't stay here if she wasn't devoted to – er – Father.' Father, Rose and the twins were the only occupants of the *Plâs* during the week, and she didn't want Rose to run away with the idea that *she* had the knack of inspiring devotion in servants. 'She's been with Father so long,' amended Angela.

None of the villagers, who being Welsh were outside the tradition of man and master, could understand this, and it said a lot about Phyllis that even in Llanelys no one could bring himself to think what is known as 'the worst'. She was a stranger in local terms. Her family had arrived fifty-odd years before, one at a time, from some-

31

where over the mountains. 'Tinkers,' said the locals contemptuously. *'Sipswn.'* Phyllis had married the local garage owner, but since he was not well-liked himself the marriage had had the effect of removing him even further from the community instead of drawing Phyllis closer. Jack was indistinguishable in the pubs from the other drinkers, and Gomer fitted unobtrusively into the loutish sub-culture that passed for youthful life in the village. But Phyllis had never been popular. She was neither a chapel-goer nor a gossip and she was suspiciously good at the tasks that other, more sensitive, people preferred not to undertake. She could strangle chickens, tend the dying, lay out the dead. And she was a much better motor mechanic than either her son or her grandson.

Rose affected to believe that Phyllis had made a pact with the Captain and would serve the funeral baked-meats from his chest, herself eating up the crumbs, together with all his sins, according to the old Welsh custom. She had an iron digestion, which had perhaps evolved to enable her to cope with her own cooking; this was of the British peasant type – watery, overboiled and unseasoned.

'She *is* ridiculous about Phyllis,' said Angela, as Rose went out for more hot water.

'She doesn't understand these people,' agreed Michael.

'Although she is one of them,' said Angela, taking a hasty bite of cherry cake as Rose returned.

*   *   *

Ermyn stood in the stable yard. The silence had the quality of new milk, fresh and heavy. She felt deaf, drowned in the opacity of quiet, anxious lest something important might be said which she wouldn't be able to hear. She was impatient and dissatisfied with herself: all her reactions were inappropriate. Other girls, she was sure, ran happily into their homes crying 'I'm back.' People came forward to meet them; dogs bounded out. Ermyn remembered the dogs. She had been frightened of them all her childhood.

The kitchen took her by surprise. It was warm and clean and ordered, the flags free of the newspaper that Phyllis had always put down for protection; stained and torn, it used to drift drearily about, far more squalid than any dirty floor. Someone had put things in their place. There was a doll's-house air of propriety and adequacy – cake on the dresser, kettle on the hob, marigolds on the table, bright enough to burn the toast. 'Rose,' said Ermyn to herself. The dogs had gone, with their nosy poking ways, claws rattling uneasily on the hard floors. Rose had thrown them all out. Even May, the bulldog, had been banished to the stables and had died – probably of a broken heart, thought Ermyn, feeling vaguely sad but not sorry. Father hadn't seemed to mind – not even when Rose had said that in future the gun room was going to be the twins' day-nursery because it was downstairs and faced south. He seemed quite glad to stay at home more, and grew cheerful before meals. In the days when Phyllis did the cooking his temper had been poor; he used to leave his plate untouched and go off for long walks to shoot something. As Ermyn grew older Father had begun to ask why she couldn't make an effort to organise the kitchen and the meals. 'Speak to Phyllis,' he'd say, as she cowered before him in her panama and blazer. 'Do something about the food.' When Rose took over the kitchen and started to cook, he said, 'That girl's got good blood from somewhere. You can always tell. It's in the bone structure.' It was lucky that Father had taken it like that, reflected Ermyn, because Rose's father had only been a horse doctor, raffish and loud: one of the Captain's drinking companions in The Goat but not a person who would ever be invited to the *Plâs*. After the wedding he had tactfully given up drinking at The Goat and taken his custom to The Bron, and after a while he and Rose's mother had tactfully died.

The kitchen smelt different now: of baking and apples and death-dealing cleaning fluids. It sounded different too. The clock was wound; it ticked bossily, finger wagging, now now now . . . Ermyn started and went into the passage that led to the hall, walking noiselessly on the sides of her feet. The drawing-room door was ajar; china rattled; there were pauses in conversation and she swallowed in sympathy. She hated tea-time: bread and butter put out hurriedly by bored au pair girls gone off to avoid her, locked in their bedrooms; eating her bread silently and in sorrow choked with loneliness and crusts, threatened by homework and the possibility that Father might be visited by a fit of interest and demand to see it; Phyllis ostentatiously caring for Gomer – 'Drink up your milk now, *cariad*.' No one had ever called Ermyn anything but Ermyn, apart from an exasperated schoolmistress who might occasionally address her as 'dear'. Tea had always been her last meal of the day. Some of the au pair girls had been cross if she hadn't eaten it all, others if she had helped herself to more . . .

She had stood for an absurdly long time outside the door. They might think she was eavesdropping.

Angela was saying, '. . . a blood row with the idiotic

34

man in the school uniform department and then after all that I got one for 2p in the jumble sale.'

Ermyn went in. Rose looked up. Perhaps she would kiss her? But Rose, although smiling, made no move, and she was kissed by Angela instead.

'You are a silly girl. We could have brought you in the car.'

Ermyn blushed. 'I travelled second class,' she said.

'I should hope so,' said Angela. 'No one travels first these days except Common Market businessmen and Japanese.'

Ermyn sat down awkwardly on a small chair just out of reach of the tea-table, so that they all had to shift slightly to see her.

'Have some tea,' said Angela.

'I'll make some more,' said Rose.

Uneasy at the prospect of being left alone with Angela and Michael so soon after arrival, Ermyn protested that she was neither hungry nor thirsty and would hate to be given tea. She knew she should ask about the children and the new house, but she couldn't. It wasn't merely that she didn't care – until she felt more settled she simply couldn't bear to be told. Angela was an insistent and demanding talker and placed pauses in her narrative so that people could nod, smile and exclaim.

'I'm not at all hungry or thirsty,' Ermyn said, as though they'd enquired about her health. Angela looked surprised and Michael tired, and Ermyn saw miserably that, as usual, she had gone too far.

'It's Ursula's party tomorrow,' said Angela, changing the subject rather obviously. 'I'm so glad we're in time.'

Ermyn's misery increased. Ursula was her godmother

and only the most watertight of excuses could save her from the party – probably nothing short of a broken leg. 'I didn't think she'd have it this year,' she said. 'Not when . . .' Her voice faded. She didn't want to sound impertinent.

'I think she's very brave,' said Angela. 'Life has to go on.'

'But . . .' said Ermyn.

'It *was* January,' said Angela.

Ursula's husband had died one dark and stormy night. His car had gone straight off the viaduct on to the bare rocks below. With him had gone the young woman, to whom – as the local paper asininely put it – he was 'giving a lift, with a kindness typical of the man.' It was difficult, observed Rose, to know which had rendered him more unrecognisable – the accident or the obituary.

Angela ignored her. 'I'm sure his death had a lot to do with Father's illness. It was a dreadful shock.'

Michael agreed. 'He was Father's oldest friend,' he said. 'The match will seem very odd without them.'

'Are you *having* the match?' asked Ermyn, before she could stop herself. She seemed fated to sound disapproving, and she felt it to be most unsuitable of her.

'Life has to go on,' said Michael. 'Father would want us to go on.'

It sounded as though he was dead already. People always said that when people died – 'He would have wanted me to have the garnets, have a ripping time, have a new husband . . .' Ermyn doubted very much whether it was so.

Angela went to the french windows and stepped into the garden. 'You should get Jack to do something about

36

this,' she remarked critically, surveying the abundant perfection of summer. The jigsaw shards of sea and sky seen through the still stops of the rhododendrons were an ancient wine-dark blue. 'It isn't at all like Welsh weather. Oh, look,' she cried with a change of tone. 'Naughty Albertine has dropped her petalcoats all over the lawn. Not enough water.' She moved on like Matron doing her rounds, palpating a sickly bud here, encouraging a limp growth there. Rose followed: Sister – observant and inimical.

Michael came up behind them. 'Girls,' he said, putting an arm round each.

Rose stooped to pull aside a trailing branch, unbalancing him.

'Spot of horticulture?' he asked. 'Angela telling you how to make the roses bloom?' He flung himself on the grass in an attitude left over from school, flat on his back, one knee bent, silly hat tipped over his eyes; he had many such clichés of gesture. He put a stalk of grass between his teeth. 'Good to be back,' he said.

In her mind's ear Rose heard the dispiriting click of cricket balls. 'How lucky you'll be here for the annual event,' she said.

'It's a pity you didn't want us to bring the children,' said Angela. 'The boys are frightfully keen. And I don't think,' she added, 'that we should try too hard to protect them from the facts of illness – it's all part of life, you know.'

Rose, whose only concern had been to protect herself from Angela's children, looked modestly at the ground. 'He doesn't recognise anyone,' she explained, 'and the twins refuse to go anywhere near him.'

Angela opened her mouth to say that the twins should be forced to see their grandfather, but thought better of it. 'That isn't the point,' she said crossly.

'Where are the twins?' asked Ermyn.

'Gone to the lake,' said Rose.

'Oh, really, Rose,' Angela bridled. 'That *is* a bit thoughtless. Cousin Dorothy must be nearly eighty and Kerrig isn't well at all.'

'They asked to have them,' explained Rose. 'They kept on writing and telephoning, so in the end I let them go.'

Angela, suddenly alert, made up her mind that as soon as she got home her children should all be made to write letters to the cousins, with drawings.

'Poor Father,' said Michael.

Ermyn glanced up from where she was sitting on the grass, and they looked at each other briefly, surprised. It had never consciously occurred to Ermyn that Michael was fond of his father. Father had always been lenient and indulgent towards the boys, but love had never taken on a discernible shape in the *Plâs*.

'I'll find Phyllis in a minute,' said Rose, 'and you can go and see him.'

Ermyn realised that she should have asked before now about her father's condition. Perhaps it would have been normal to burst in, distraught, with the anguished enquiry on her lips. She shuffled uneasily. Father's absence was as startling as his presence, his silence as alarming as his voice.

'It must have been a shock,' she said.

'Oh, it was,' said Rose. The biggest shock had been to the village drunk, quietly downing another pint when the

Captain fell in it. The barmaid from The Goat had told her all about it next day in the village. 'Damn,' he'd said, leaping up and wringing out his trousers. 'Who's going to pay for that, then? Damn.' And the poor Captain, lying there like a log in the broken glass and the bar stools. There was something in the way the barmaid from The Goat told this tale that made Rose laugh. They had both laughed. Shamed, they had hidden in the alleyway next to the post office, laughing and pretending to admire the roses that drooped down its toadflax-studded walls.

'We mustn't give up hope,' said Angela. 'He has a splendid constitution.'

*　　*　　*

Phyllis was giving Jack and Gomer their tea in the kitchen.

'*Sut dach i*, Jack, Gomer,' cried Michael in the vernacular.

Jack half rose, pushing the end of a piece of bread into his mouth. 'Evening, squire,' he said and sat down again.

Gomer didn't move. He grinned his stupid, knowing grin and went on chewing.

'Twins all right?' asked Rose casually. Jack bore no sign of violence or disaster and he wouldn't be calmly eating corned beef like that if they were lying dead by the roadside somewhere. The ghostly umbilical tension eased. Even the fresh trail of sheep droppings outside the kitchen door failed to annoy her as much as usual.

'We've had a visitor,' said Angela behind her.

39

'Virginia Woolf,' said Rose.

The sheep had been named because of the facial resemblance, which was very marked.

'We always called the house-lamb Megan,' said Michael.

'She eats the snapdragons,' said Rose. 'It's Ermyn's fault. She kept feeding her bits of bread and butter at Easter and now she comes to ravage the herbaceous border.'

Ermyn jumped remorsefully. 'She was so sweet,' she said. At Easter the lamb had seemed to have a sacred Paschal quality, tripping delicately over the dead golden mountain grass, round the mounds of crystalline snow, coming down honouring her with its tameness, its willingness to share her food.

'Well, I wouldn't worry about the herbaceous border,' said Angela tolerantly. 'They went out years ago.'

'They've come back,' said Rose. She parted the cool hydrangea heads and peered into the spiritless interior of the shrubbery.

'She must have gone this way,' said Ermyn over a tuft of decapitated pansies. She put the tip of her finger into the mouth of a yellow snapdragon and it bit her, gently, reluctantly, with soft vegetable lips.

'I've mended that fence often enough,' called Jack the Liar from the kitchen table as he waited for his mother to pour him another cup of tea.

'Oh, indeed you have,' said Rose. But it wasn't Jack she was angry with. There was something about the animal's calm assumption of equal and simultaneous rights over the gardens that irked her disproportionately.

'Seriously, Rose,' Angela went on, 'this should be a

40

mountain garden. You want heather and bluebells and a conifer or two.'

Rose looked round. Hadn't Angela noticed? Behind them lay great cushions of heather just turning purple. In the turf that showed between grew harebells and scabious and inside the boundary fence stood three enormous pines.

'Time to see the Captain,' said Phyllis peremptorily.

'Roll up, roll up,' said Rose under her breath.

There was, at this moment, something of the showman about Phyllis. She led them indoors, keeping ahead.

Rose wandered along the path that justified her herbaceous border. It led from the back of the house to the front and was intended to ease the strangeness of the contrast. The transition was gradual – from the greys and greens of an old Welsh farmhouse, past the clumps of ugly pink valerian and the flowering currant, under the wall of the house, until, the first clue to change, a mass of fuchsia bushes hung with dancing ladies flourishing wildly. On the left lay a small patch of grass, the drying lawn, half-concealed by feral shrubs and writhen bushes of lavender and sage. It was seldom used now; Phyllis fed the clothes to a machine every Monday and they came out clean and dry. Below the lavender a slate path trailed round and down beside the high garden wall to the lower gate, and in front of the house lay the proper, planned gardens: a broad grass terrace that fell abruptly down a slope cut with shallow steps, a wide lawn, and below that another bounded all round by hedges and trees, dense as enchantment. It was much as it had been all those years ago when the Captain's mother had laid it out in the modern mode. Llanelys then had been a prosperous little watering place

41

for the well-to-do, and the fashion had been for the marine and the exotic. Graceful, murderous groups of sword grass and dwarf palms bore witness to it. A small bamboo plantation struggled not to lose face against the native alders and willows that grew along the boundary stream. There was a pond in the lower lawn, slimily green and lilied over. It had been full of goldfish that swam in idle circles, until one winter a passing heron had eaten them all. The conservatory had been pulled down in the war, but unidentified things still sprang up around the site. Rose was particularly fond of the monkey puzzle that grew by the lower gate: a constant affront to the family, having acquired over the years a suburban image of respectability which vexed them – the respectability of the bank manager or dentist. Rose insisted that this was merely because it had been plagiarised by people who knew no better. Looked at with the eyes of innocence, the tree and the gardens had an arcane charm. The roses and honeysuckle swarming tomboyishly out of control up the dark poplars only added to it. It was as though the fish-tailed tennis rackets had just been put away and the fairy lights dimmed.

On the right of the upper lawn the hens were strutting about in their low run screened by little trees – apple and quince and greengage. They were elegant black hens with yellow beaks and legs, and they went with the front of the house rather than with the back: had there been room for a run on the drying lawn, Rose would have chosen fat red hens with the usual banal, cosy farmyard character. They flocked to see if Rose was bringing them something to eat and walked away again disgustedly. 'On the contrary,' she said coldly to an importunate fowl pecking through the wire mesh at a grain of corn. It had stopped laying and Phyllis had agreed to kill it.

Rose returned by the left to the back of the house. The terrace swerved round, up the slope, and escaped under the wire fence to where the garden merged imperceptibly into the mountain. Behind the dairy and the outhouses the atmosphere was quite different – civilised, but to other requirements, by people whose fantastic imaginings had kept them indoors after dark, behind small deep-set windows built to keep out the weather. They had had to wrest their living from the mountain and had little interest in its scenic aspects. When the family took over the house as a permanent residence – it had previously been only the *hafod*, the place where their shepherds stayed in the summer months to give the sheep the benefit of the mountain grass and the wild thyme – they left it as it was and made extra, larger and airier rooms around and above it. Each generation had added something. The old shepherds would hardly recognise it now with its tall windows and its pretty gardens and its general air of warmth and leisure. They had had to contend with the mountain walker, the nebulous giant who came with the evening to take men, and the ghosts who lurked at crossroads and gateways, and they must always have been tired – until the corpse candle or a loud unearthly knocking in the night warned them that the end was near. They had been superstitious people, seeing signs and portents in everything. Rose wondered what the light could have been that appeared before the door of those about to die and whether it would come soon to glimmer in front of the *Plâs*.

She slid down the narrow space between the stable and the gateway and crossed the yard to the kitchen door. The

43

room was empty. She began to move things about, preparing supper.

Upstairs Ermyn found herself the first to go into the sickroom. The light was muted by sheets joined across the windows, but every detail of the room was clearly visible – more so than usual with the absence of any distracting reflection or gleam. There was no movement. Even the afternoon, so vital in the garden, seemed to have stopped breathing in here. Father lay more still than the furniture. He looked very serious. Ermyn had seen that look before. It was entirely familiar; she had no need to strain her memory. Father's face had the sobriety of a newborn child's, a dreadful sobriety, at once pitiful and disturbing. The twins had looked like that before they learned to smile, when their lives had seemed compounded of greed and grief. Unsmiling, they had seemed infinitely wise and infinitely disapproving, like the worst sort of god. When they were fed they either screamed or went to sleep, with never a sign of thanks or appreciation; but they had moved with sudden starts and nuzzlings. Father did nothing. At most his expression deepened from consideration to anxiety, like a baby with wind. He plainly couldn't see the funny side to anything, nor did his situation strike him as incongruous. He was settled in it, as only the totally dependent can be. The twins had become human when they learned to smile – had shed infinity.

Ermyn grinned around at everyone, encouraging them to help.

'*Ermyn.*'

But she was less mortified by her own absurdity than by the fact that no one was really surprised.

Michael kept his eyes on the bedhead. It was heavily carved and ornamented; faces formed and faded among the leaves and acorns; there was a bunch of curling, crisping mint tied to one of the knobs. He looked helplessly at Angela, who was never at a loss; but she was talking seriously to Phyllis by the window. He looked back at the silent figure on the bed and quickly away. It had a shrunken, detumescent look, indefinably obscene. Death did not suit the Captain.

Angela was, in fact, at a loss. Phyllis was uncommunicative, possessive, not prepared to share a single detail of the Captain's plight. The usual attitude to invalids was inappropriate here. It was impossible to give that oblivious object orders – 'You have a nice rest now', 'You look after yourself', 'You get better soon and don't worry about a thing'. It would have been all right if she and Michael had been there alone. She could have smoothed the sheets, glanced at her watch, wondered about the temperature of the room. As it was, she was denied all function; and the role of onlooker was distasteful to her.

'Come on now,' said Phyllis, the show over.

They went out obediently, inadequate and obscurely dissatisfied. Phyllis closed the bedroom door.

'He really ought to be in hospital,' said Angela. Suddenly Michael sniffed and she brightened. 'It is dreadful to see him like that,' she said compassionately. She put her arm through her husband's and felt for a handkerchief in his pocket. Good in a crisis, she tugged at him. 'Let's go and see where Henry's hidden the brandy.'

*   *   *

45

'How long can you stay?' asked Rose carefully.

Angela put a finger to her cheek and thought. 'Not too long. Mother is marvellous,' she said, 'but she's not a young woman and the children are very lively . . . We'll help all we can, of course.'

'There isn't anything to do,' said Rose. 'Jack helps Phyllis with the Captain and Gomer does this and that.'

'He should have a proper job,' said Angela.

'Phyllis won't let him,' said Rose. 'Her life revolves around him. She dotes on him.'

Michael glanced up uneasily. It was odd that the lower classes should be thought of as loving each other. Surely their love and devotion, insofar as they were capable of such refinement of feeling, were due to their employers and betters. That was the way life was ordered.

'Very bad for him,' said Angela firmly. 'Anyway, it's really too much for Phyllis. If Father can't be moved, you must get a nurse. I'll talk to Henry about it. What time will he be back?'

'I don't know,' said Rose. 'Late. He's having dinner with some people.' Henry never interfered in the running of the household. Angela was not immediately dangerous, but she carried the possibility of harm – like a door left open on a windy day.

'I'll help you get supper,' Angela said.

'Thanks,' said Rose with no perceptible irony.

Ermyn coming into the hall heard the drawing-room door open and went hurriedly into the study. Father had spent a lot of time in here smoking and drinking. The big leather chair still bore his imprint. She stared at it. It seemed to her that there should be a sort of ambulant hole in the fabric of things, that a space of a shape to

accommodate Father should be wandering the house backwards – that death should be not a mere change but a
total reversal . . .

This room too had been subjected to alteration in the
30s, but the fireplace which until recently had aroused
nothing but hatred and contempt now looked quite at
home. It was surrounded by plum-coloured tiles with a
black border and was really rather nicely proportioned.
It was like modern art, thought Ermyn: after a while,
when you got used to it, it reminded you of itself. That was
the point of art, that it should remind you of something.
Everything reminded Ermyn of something. She purposely
didn't look at the painting over the fireplace. It was a
melancholy picture of a dead duck hanging upside down
and bleeding from the beak on to an overflowing charger
of fruit, with a brace of hares, likewise defunct, lying to its
right.

The shelves were full of books, unopened since the
death of the last literate forebear. Father had added a
sentimental story about a goose which a lady had given
him – it had moved him very much and constituted a
strong bond between them, adding an intellectual dimen-
sion to their relationship – and the works of Churchill.
The village electrician, who was often up at the *Plás*
tinkering with the defective wiring, always left this room
in a dark and vengeful mood. Like all Welshmen of his
generation he was well-read and versed in history and
politics; he had a long memory, and was quite unable to
forgive Mr Churchill for what he had done to the miners
at Tonypandy.

The books had their backs to her and Ermyn felt
snubbed. The whole room had a still, unwelcoming feel-

47

ing, as though it was waiting for her to leave before it could relax and be itself – the books would fall open a little, the picture sag on its rope, the chair expand . . . 'Excuse me,' mouthed Ermyn, backing out as quietly as she could and closing the oak door. The drawing-room doors opposite were made of mahogany and had a friendly Edwardian air. They looked indulgent – doors to let people in – but the black oak door behind was secretive and close: a door to keep people out. Ermyn sensed it bracing itself more firmly against the jamb.

The kitchen was cool and swept, the blue shadows thickening. Rose turned on the lamp that stood on the dresser and Ermyn felt better at once. The Devil, who presided over the afternoon and the tea table, took his leave, as a more necessary, more convivial event became imminent. The ingredients of a proper meal lay illuminated on the kitchen table: bowls of potatoes and lettuce, half a wheel of cheese. Knives and wooden spoons were laid out neatly.

'Heavens,' said Angela, displeased. 'How efficient.'

'We'll eat in the kitchen,' said Rose, slicing onions with skill and precision. 'Jack and Gomer can go home or somewhere.'

There was an unpleasant sound of braking in the yard and Jack appeared with Ermyn's suitcase as though summoned. He saw at once what the situation was and removed his ingratiating smile.

'Oh, thank you, Jack,' said Ermyn.

'Good *night*,' said Jack.

Angela looked round for something to do.

'You could carve the ham,' said Rose, who did not like doing this.

'You needn't have gone to all this trouble our first night. We could have had bread and cheese.'

'You are,' said Rose, 'with ham and salad.' She eyed the gleaming knife blade and reflected on the crassness which passes with the English for common sense.

*　　*　　*

Henry arrived late. He was not alone.

'He's brought the dog,' said Rose.

'Who?' asked Angela.

'His friend Edward,' said Rose. 'He's a respected and distinguished journalist, but you won't believe it.'

'Oh, *that* Edward,' said Angela. 'He was at school with Michael.' She assumed a pretty, feminine position and prepared her mouth to smile. He was really quite famous, and his views were similar to her own. Her friends often quoted him to each other approvingly.

'His wife tried to kill him a few months ago,' explained Rose. 'So he gets away whenever he can. Mostly here.'

'Oh rubbish, Rose,' said Angela, still about to smile. She gazed expectantly at the kitchen door.

Ermyn stared at it too. When it opened another change would have taken place. She thought how peaceful it would be to be a nun in an enclosed order where nothing had changed for hundreds of years and never would, she thought, being unfamiliar with the current upheavals in the Roman Church. When the door opened only Henry was visible, filling up a space designed with themselves in mind by smaller Welshmen. A few stars gleamed by each of his ears.

'Hello,' said Rose.

49

Ermyn told herself reasonably that it was nice that Henry was home. Cigar smoke and men's voices added something to a house. Henry was now really head of the household and his presence was right and reassuring. But by the slight dull misery behind her eyes she knew she was untruthful. The evening, which had been leading down gently to sleep, revived unnaturally.

'Drink, Edward?' said Henry, pushing aside the jug of marigolds, as he looked for the glasses, which were kept on the dresser. His coat sleeve caught a small saucer and knocked it to the floor, where it rang for a moment before it broke.

'Fish fingers,' said Angela, laughing.

'Damn,' said Henry casually, sweeping away the pieces with his foot. Ermyn leapt forward, picked them up and stacked them tidily on a corner of the range.

Edward stood by the table sipping whisky and water. Ermyn watched him, thinking of snails. He was small. He wore round bottle-bottom glasses, and his head was no wider than his neck. There was about him the faintest suggestion of slime.

'I'm sorry, Rose.' He smiled a little nervously. 'Henry said you wouldn't mind.'

'Your bed's still made up,' said Rose.

'Is it aired?' asked Angela. 'I'd better fill some hotties.'

'It's only been a week,' said Rose.

Angela pulled her chair a little nearer to Edward. 'Michael will be pleased you're here. He went to bed early. I think seeing his papa like that was a bit of a shock.'

Edward looked grave at this reminder of the family's sorrow. 'I was Henry's contemporary,' he said; 'but I can just remember Michael. He was a rather small boy.'

'You'll find he's grown a lot,' said Rose. 'These days he's something nasty in the City.'

'He *was* small as a boy,' said Angela. 'But then he put on a spurt and he's nearly as tall as Henry.'

'He's a bit bandy,' said Rose. 'I expect he had rickets. So many upper-middle-class kiddies did, because their nannies fed them on rice pudding and boiled cod.'

'Fiddlesticks, Rose,' said Angela. 'He's as straight as a die. And they didn't,' she added. 'Does your wife write too?' she asked Edward, hoping to discover by this means the true state of his feelings about his marriage. She didn't believe Rose's version.

'She used to,' he said rather abruptly. He was unwilling to discuss his marriage in front of Rose since it made her laugh. For some reason he had married a small but powerful and foul-tempered Scot with pretty, vicious features, a great mass of hair and a tendency to give way to intermittent fits of drunken violence. Her life, she was wont to tell him, was centred in her children, of whom there were three, and she didn't give a damn for anyone else – not *anyone*, d'ye hear.

'Did she write for a daily paper?' needled Angela.

'For a while,' said Edward. 'Did it take you long to get here? The roads were . . .'

It was too late. 'She was a cub reporter,' said Rose joyously. 'She told me so. A little glossy, fluffy, sweet little cub reporter – till she turned rabid.'

'She's very highly strung,' said Edward, 'but they've just started her on a new pill. They're very hopeful.'

Angela spoke to him for a while about the strides made by medicine in the field of nervous illness.

Henry looked unusually sombre.

51

'What's the matter?' asked Rose, surprised, thinking it unlikely that he was worrying about Edward's mad wife.

'Rabies,' said Henry. 'Fatty Phil took his dog to France and back. Just sailed over, let it ashore and then sailed back.'

'I hope you told the police,' said Angela, interrupting herself in the middle of a story about a friend of her mother's who had had electric shock treatment and felt much better. 'How on earth did he get past the customs?'

'They don't go through customs. They just sail up to empty stretches of coast and have picnics.'

'*Sail?*' asked Angela.

'In his yacht,' said Edward. 'Fatty Phil bought himself a yacht and he's organising a club.'

Angela stared at him, her eyes wide open. 'Yacht club?' she said. 'A yacht club in *Llanelys?* How frightfully funny. Who *is* Fatty Phil?'

'He owns the newsagent's shop,' explained Rose.

'Oh goodness,' cried Angela, falling about decorously. 'Imagine. The Llanelys yacht club.' The Captain's father had belonged to the real yacht club over the straits, world-famous for its tone. 'You *must* tell the coastguard or the police.'

'Rabies is a terrible thing,' said Rose, reflectively. 'My father knew. He observed it in the war when he was travelling. Just the sight of a drink would put the poor creatures into a spasm so dreadful no one could hold them. They'd foam at the mouth and tear into tiny pieces anyone who dared come near them . . .'

'For heaven's sake, Rose,' said Angela, putting down her whisky. '*Must* you?'

'Never mind,' said Rose. 'Rabies is horrible, but werewolves were worse, and you needn't worry about them any more because they're the same thing. My father noticed.'

'I'm not afraid of werewolves,' said Angela.

'Yes, you are,' said Rose. 'Everyone is. But werewolves were only people in the final rabid stages. The muscular spasms that gripped them made them savagely strong and the dreadful pain and fear brought them down to their hands and knees, and the muscles of their faces snarled right back, and they frothed most copiously for fear of being drowned in their own spit, and anything that might make them swallow – like holy water, or garlic that might make them salivate – threw them into the most ghastly terror, so people thought they were possessed. See?'

'No,' said Angela.

'They behaved like animals,' said Henry. 'Mad animals.'

'And they could truly be described as *dangerously* ill,' said Rose. 'It is very infectious.' At this she remembered the twins' fondness for dogs – they were given to embracing them, kissing them on their snouts . . .

'Bed,' said Henry. 'It's been a long day.'

'It seemed to me,' said Rose, 'about average.' But she didn't stay to argue. She took the glasses down the steps to the scullery and rinsed them at the sink. She seldom used the machines which Henry had bought to make her life easy. Electricity behaved badly to Rose: plugs exploded at her touch with a rude and shocking violence, engines ground shuddering to a halt, and in the ease with which the modern conveniences performed their domestic tasks was a measure of contempt, a dumb insolence. They

53

never apologised if they shrank the clothes or curdled the sauce. Electric power without responsibility. Phyllis, on the other hand, used the machines, mastering them with an insensitive confidence greater than their own.

Rose frowned at the night-steeled window over the sink. Her face shone palely in it, her black hair merging into the blackness. For a moment she seemed to herself weak and defenceless. It was an unusual sensation. She opened her mouth and breathed heartily at the glass until it was clouded over.

On her way to her bedroom she passed the door at the foot of the flight of stairs that led to the attics and turned the handle to make sure it was locked. No one ever went up there. She hadn't herself until she'd changed Angela's bedroom and Jack and Gomer had hauled up the furniture groaning and sweating. She had gone along to see fair play and was surprised at the extent and variety of the objects that were uncovered to make way for the mahogany. Now she went there quite often to refresh her sense of knowledge and power.

Phyllis was still up, talking to herself in the dressing-room next to the Captain's where she slept. Rose, who also sometimes talked to herself, wondered a little uneasily whether perhaps she and Phyllis were not rather alike. She shivered and went quickly into her bedroom, closing the door hastily and loudly.

*   *   *

Rose woke early, with her confidence quite restored, and chose her clothes carefully. On her way downstairs she came across Ermyn leaning out of the landing window gazing and sniffing. The morning had dawned as soft and clear as pale blue silk. Wild roses and honeysuckle hung against it, timeless and still as a printed pattern. Even the sea lay like a discarded petticoat, delicately tucked and frilled.

'What are you doing, Ermyn?' asked Rose.

Ermyn started. 'Oh,' she said. 'I didn't hear you.' She was thinking that the day would have made a dress for a young mother – so tender, so soft and blue. 'I was looking for Virginia Woolf,' she said. 'To see if she was eating the dahlias. We'll eat *her* one day,' she went on merrily. 'Roast her shoulders and legs and stew her ribs.'

Rose looked at her sideways. Ermyn's spasmodic jocularities were always unnerving. 'Well, don't overbalance,' she said.

'Unbalanced?' cried Ermyn. 'Not me.'

'I said, you'll fall out,' said Rose.

'Oh, we will,' said Ermyn; 'if you talk to me like that.' She laughed aloud and ran gaily down the stairs, across the hall and out into the garden, still unaware, like the rest of her family, that the measles she had caught as a little girl, which had been unrecognised and untreated until she had almost disappeared beneath the converging spots, had left her slightly but permanently deaf.

Downstairs Rose found Gomer sitting at the kitchen table, knife poised over a fried egg as though he was about to carve his name on it.

'Good morning, Gomer,' she said.

Phyllis paused by his chair defensively. 'More bread, *cariad*?' she asked him.

'More cake?' suggested Rose. Evidence of an earlier repast lay on the table – a half-empty orangeade bottle

55

and a box that had held four factory-made jam tarts.

'Got to keep him fed,' said Phyllis in obscure warning. 'He was up at six.'

Gomer grinned eggily. He was a short, solid boy, scarlet-haired and pink-lipped. His face and arms were pink too, and freckled and damp, and he had always looked as though he drank, even before he could walk. He gestured at her with his knife, and Rose turned away. A little while before she had realised that Gomer imagined the prospect of sexual congress between them to be not impossibly remote. He crept along the flower borders to peer up her skirt, tried to brush against her as he brought in the milk and the logs. Rose treated him with cold and immaculate contempt, which he obviously regarded as assumed. He was like a stupid and unattractive puppy, incapable of recognising rebuff, and Rose wished someone would beat him with a chain.

She began to clear the table pointedly.

Phyllis, who tacitly agreed the boundaries, patted her grandson's shoulder. 'Good boy,' she said.

He left unwillingly, taking a slice of bread and butter to eat on the way.

Phyllis stood at the kitchen door and watched until he had gone out of the gateway. She was unsmiling when she turned, and her heart was not in her work. It was plain to anyone who thought about it that she considered Gomer to be her own child and his mother of no more relevance or significance than a railway station or post office. Anyway, to Jack's great relief the Spanish girl had disappeared almost immediately after the birth. Jack had nearly collapsed when she turned up, six months gone and looking for him. He remembered her vaguely. He'd

56

met her at a holiday camp where she was working as a waitress, but as he was quite sure he'd told her no more than that his name was Jones and he came from Wales her reappearance had smacked of the supernatural. Of course, when she had left it was suggested that Jack had murdered her and dropped her in Elys Water, but no one really believed it: he was not a violent man. The village had been more shocked by Phyllis's attitude. She hadn't even bothered to hint at a quiet wedding some months previously. The locals were accustomed to very large premature babies tightly wrapped in swaddling clothes and hidden in the shade of pram hoods. The other proud but proper grannies, pushing down the inappropriately alert, sometimes even speaking, head, would explain that, yes, he was a big boy for two weeks but it ran in the family. Phyllis hadn't even been brazen. She hadn't seemed to mind, carrying the baby around everywhere she went, her large face weak with tenderness, her eyes lowered to where he lay.

Phyllis sighed and began to warm up the Captain's breakfast, a light-grey unappealing form of nourishment which she would feed to him, spoonful by spoonful, without interest. The Captain, after all, would not now grow into a lovely boy.

Angela wandered wearily into the kitchen. 'Llanelys is enervating,' she said plaintively. 'It's always a few days till one gets used to it. Michael's still asleep.' She had opened her eyes to the green-and-beige bedroom and wondered where on earth she was. She looked resentfully at Rose. 'I think I'll just have a little piece of toast.'

Rose turned up the grill. 'The doctor will be here soon. He comes every day about now.'

'Good,' said Angela. 'I want to talk to him.' She sat down at the kitchen table and looked at the thick white china which stood on it. Really. You could never tell with Rose – drawing-room tea one moment and lorryman's caff the next. She supposed it was her upbringing.

Edward opened the door and ushered in Ermyn. Angela glanced quickly from one to the other and then smiled at herself reproachfully . . . As if Ermyn, as if Edward . . .

'I was walking in the garden,' said Edward, 'and I found this young lady about to jump into the fishpond.'

'I wasn't,' said Ermyn. She suspected that Edward meant to be kind, but his efforts were mistaken and sounded more like teasing. She'd been balancing on the stone rim of the pond to a count of 19 and was aware that she must have looked foolish. It was a rite left over from childhood, designed to avert misfortune, and Edward had interrupted her. 'I was looking at the newts,' she said. 'Some are black and some are green and they live in the pond.'

There was a silence.

'I'll heat up some coffee,' said Angela, rising with energetic grace from her chair. 'Phyllis, don't clear the table yet.'

Phyllis looked put out. She glanced at Edward with a distasteful incomprehension – as though he was caviar, thought Rose, or some foreign stuff with garlic. She whispered this to Ermyn, who laughed quietly at the back of her nose.

'Don't honk, Ermyn,' said Angela. 'Boil yourself an egg if you want one. Alexander made me a machine to boil eggs in,' she told Edward. 'He's only ten and it actually works – it's got a battery and an arm to put them in and a gadget to . . .'

Edward didn't even look bored, thought Ermyn. He must be falling in love with her. She grimaced.

'Don't make faces, Ermyn. Eat your breakfast and go and get some sun – you're dreadfully pasty. Edward, one egg or two?'

'Two please,' said Edward.

*   *   *

Rose sat on the wide slate step edged with brass that shone unbearably in the morning sun. She was waiting for the doctor, who was a nice old man but easily swayed. The rest of the village preferred his younger partner, on the grounds that the old man was a killer; but the family remained loyal, encouraged by Rose, who was still punishing the younger partner for falling in love with her at the age of thirteen when he was at school with her brothers. He had expressed his passion by throwing stones at her – the sharp gravel chippings that abounded in the district – and she had a small triangular scar on the calf of her left leg to this very day. Moreover he held that the Captain should keep to a strict cholesterol-free diet, and Rose wasn't having that. 'People of his age,' she said with great conviction, 'need nourishment.'

The old doctor treated the Captain efficiently and without fuss. There was no chance of recovery and no point in taking the Captain away, and the doctor admitted it without professional pride or officiousness. Nevertheless, thought Rose, it would be wise to keep Angela from him. The Captain should die here in his own house – not for

59

his sake, but for the house's. Without events it would grow vacuous and stale and lose the true definition of its purpose.

The doctor was in a hurry. 'Oh Anthea,' he said to Angela, who was waiting in the hall. 'Nice to see you. You're looking well.'

*   *   *

Goodhumouredly, Rose said Ermyn could come shopping with her. The day still had that silken perfection, gentle and cool, and the steep lane was dappled with golden light. There was a heartbreaking smell of new-mown hay – contingent on the labours of man and doomed to die with him, like the smell of bread and incense. Ermyn felt tears at the corners of her eyes and sniffed. If they met anyone, perhaps they'd think she was crying for Father and be pleased with her.

Ashamed of this thought, Ermyn shook her head. It was silly to cry for things you couldn't help and she would shortly have to brace herself for the housing estate. Already they were passing occasional bungalows perched behind the hedges on the bank above. Steps led up to them, stopping at wooden gates shaped like the rising sun, or iron gates bent like hairpins, behind which snarled large hostile dogs. In Llanelys the size of the dogs was in inverse proportion to the social status of their owners, except for poodles of course – the hairdresser and the barmaid from The Goat each had one of these. The doctor's wife had two miniature dachshunds like unwrapped toffees and the solicitor kept a Jack Russell terrier, while the parvenus kept alsatians and labradors and enormous Afghan hounds. Father's attitude to these people and their habitations was strange – he was hardly aware of them, rather as Zulus accustomed to living in round huts are said to be unable to recognise the angular proportions of Western architecture.

Phyllis's bungalow seemed almost to leap at them as they came to it past another gap in the hedge. It was made of shiny, unvariegated brick and looked horrifyingly, angrily red – perhaps with embarrassment at being so out of place among the old fields and sheep roads. Inside, it had that uniquely rural squalor which results from the attempt to impose urban notions of 'luxury' on quite unsuitable surroundings. There were odd squares and strips of auction-sale carpet, fouled with mud and chicken droppings, on the sweating, tiled floors. Nylon and dingy brocade curtains hid the windows. Pieces of torn linoleum with a pattern of wet pebbles lay under the sink superimposed on an older, brown and disintegrating floor-covering. Stone-patterned wallpaper was peeling away round the fireplace and there were several more types of wallpaper on the other walls. The rooms were barely traversable for the amount of furniture they contained: cocktail cabinets, three-piece suites, bedroom suites – the dressing-table set firmly before the window, keeping out the light and revealing its rough warped back to the passers-by – electric fires, pouffes and awful pictures of charging elephants, weeping children and the Boul. Mich. in summer with sunshades. Jack had bought these at the closing sale of a furniture store and liked to expound on their subtlety of execution and depth of perception.

Now they were passing some big houses which stood in their own gardens, decently veiled by trees and ivy

61

and without the forced bonhomie of open-plan living. Ermyn knew by sight some of the people who lived here and even some of their names, but the Captain was the only one of his kind in Llanelys and none was a close friend. One of the houses had been taken over as a home for the backward, who gathered meekly outside each morning waiting for a special bus which took them off to a place where they made baskets. The villagers and Father were extremely suspicious of them. Father would have preferred them not to exist, not to be waiting around for their bus, smiling and starting disjointedly; but they aroused in Ermyn a hot and tearful tenderness which she knew Father would deplore.

'Did you hear?' Rose asked, 'that when the duchess opened the home she inspired such a fever of loyalty and enthusiasm that five of the patients and one of the staff had fits and had to be given skilled treatment.'

Now they were coming to the building site, where architects had expressed themselves. Father had sold the land to developers and Ermyn felt she would never understand why: he was not a poor man and he was quite unconcerned about the homeless. One year moles had thrown up earthy little hillocks all over the lower lawn. 'Looks like the beginnings of a council estate,' Father had said disgustedly. It was beyond her comprehension. Half-completed chalets in different shades of artificial stone and varnished wood stood on shallow muddy terraces. Some were finished and named – Chaparral, Ericanivy, Yorjoy. And scattered around them were tricycles, plaster gnomes and geraniums.

'Don't look,' advised Rose.

'Who lives there?' asked Ermyn. She was puzzled by

something in Rose's voice. It was almost satisfaction.

'I don't know,' said Rose. 'There's no work. All the shops are closing. I don't know who lives there.'

'I suppose the people who live in them like them,' said Ermyn tremulously, looking determinedly before her. Violets and wild strawberries had grown in that field once, and the ewes with their lambs had found it comforting after the winds on the hills.

They emerged from the lane on to a wider road and were faced by the English Congregational church. The church proper – the Church in Wales – lay five hundred yards away, and Ebenezer stood on the right almost in the village. There were five other chapels in occasional use, and one that had been transformed into a milk-packing station. The Catholic church was on the top road with a small convent of enclosed nuns behind it. Ermyn tried to imagine living on the top road and never walking along it, gazing forever into the lap of the mountain. She found the thought appealing.

Rose pulled her sharply to the extreme edge of the road as a car sped past. There were no pavements here and the holiday drivers seemed unaware of the existence of such creatures as pedestrians.

'Road hog,' remarked Rose. She flexed her fingers fastidiously.

'I suppose they've got to have holidays,' said Ermyn, sliding along by the wall as car after car shot past. There was very little variety in the occupants of the cars – two adults, two children and one dog, or a middle-aged couple with a friend and sometimes two dogs, sometimes not. It was minimally safer in the village, as long as you didn't attempt to cross the road. It was the main coast road and all the drivers on it were already in a temper because of the traffic jam at the bridge behind them. Released from it they put their feet down. Fathers of families, drivers of buses and lorries had but one thing in mind, to get to their destination. Behind them on the road there were accidents. Survivors knelt bleeding and distraught begging someone to stop and aid them, but no one stopped. Singlemindedly the motorists swept by on the other side, causing further accidents.

The pavements were crowded with many more of the sort of visitors Ermyn had observed on the train. They were still unsmiling and had the air of people determined to make the most of what they could get and not have anything put over on them. The shopkeepers, on the other hand, smiling like spiders, were determined to gain every last drop of nourishment from the seasonal swarm. Ermyn felt a little reassured as she saw a family of tall people, tastefully clad in faded denim. These were their own sort. But as they passed she heard them speaking in some foreign tongue which she supposed to be Norwegian.

Rose and Ermyn picked their way along between the grey-and-white bodies in summer frocks and anoraks, bathing costumes and trousers with straps under the instep, open-necked shirts and nylon shorts. They were halted by a large group of people in front of a rack of filthy postcards and had to back into a shop to get past. Two lay nuns were buying pencils. They wore short dresses and cardigans, and their colourless, unwholesome hair stuck angularly out beneath the table napkins they now wore instead of veils. Once, when you went out you could hope to see at least a few beautiful people in ample shapely robes, veils lifting on the wind – real clothes, with the significance clothes should have: reassuring, decisive. Now nuns were the ugliest people on the street, ugly as unfed fledgling birds.

'It's because they think all beauty has sexual connotations,' said Rose. 'They say it's because the modern world demands a greater degree of practicality, but it's really the new puritanism which holds the Church in its clammy clutches. From a practical point of view it was in the Middle Ages that they should have had short skirts – all that muck on the roads. *And,*' she added, 'I've seen a nun in lipstick. So the confusion in their poor minds is pitiable. Horrible,' she said, as they reached the shoe-repairers at the end of the narrow, glass-roofed arcade. 'Ugh, horrible.'

Ermyn had to agree. Looked at in the mass, the visitors were worse. Their weight was curiously unevenly distributed. Most were far too fat, but some were emaciatedly thin. They were all somehow misshapen and they were all eating – lollies, ices, sweets, crisps, scotch eggs, cornish pasties and rock.

'Sodom and Gomorrah,' said Rose.

She turned into the greengrocers and Ermyn followed.

'Plaice, please,' said Rose, 'as long as it was caught this morning and hasn't been to Billingsgate and back, and a pound of unsalted butter.' The greengrocer, in the general lust for money, had taken to selling fish, as well as tinned goods and lengths of Welsh flannel.

'We need marmalade,' said Rose, as they left the shop, and Ermyn turned automatically to Jones & Sons, the high-class grocers, who stocked the delicacies Father liked – pâté and Dundee cake with whisky in it.

But the shop was closed, the broad marble counters empty and dusty. A poster advertising last year's sheep-dog trials hung limply by one corner in the fly-blown window.

'It got to be too much for him,' explained Rose of 'young' Mr Jones. 'They found him lying behind the counter, flat on his back, and took him away.' The lady in the baby-linen shop who sold buckets and spades had a drink problem too and closed early every day.

'I get marmalade from the antique shop,' said Rose. Here they sold modern hand-thrown pottery and soft toys, made in Czechoslovakia.

The stationer next door was doing well. He sold sweets and ice-creams, paperbacks with bleeding nudes on the covers and another sort of pottery – jam-pots shaped like beehives, or castles made in Stoke-on-Trent and inscribed 'A Present from Llanelys'. Most days the owner left his assistants to sell these things and went off sailing around in his little yacht.

The bookshop had become a cake shop, where they sold soft drinks and sheepskins; and the cake shop was now a launderette, where they did television repairs on the side.

The hairdresser was prospering. She had bought up the chemist next door and expanded her salon to include a coffee machine and a magazine bar.

'You will notice,' said Rose as they threaded their way along, 'that we no longer have anywhere that sells real bread. People who don't bake have to go thirty miles for a decent loaf.'

They were jostled by a group of teenagers and Ermyn stepped back on to the foot of a small man wearing only a pair of trousers, above which the top of his underpants was visible, and a tam-o'-shanter. His torso was greyish and streaky, like the raw pastry that Rose sometimes gave to the twins to play with. He glared at her, outraged.

'I am sorry,' said Ermyn. 'Oh, I am so sorry.'

Something about her voice seemed to madden the small man.

'Think you're something. Think you own the earth, doncha?'

He pushed her aside and strode off, muttering.

* * *

The relief Ermyn felt when they'd climbed back up the lane and pushed open the door in the high wall was so great that for a moment she mistook it for happiness. The garden kept out the sound of the visitors and the traffic, and the dust. The concrete mixers and the housing estate were a million miles away. 'It is good to be home,' she said.

They found Edward and Angela sitting in front of the house.

Angela greeted them animatedly. She wore, Rose noticed, the pink, pleased expression of a woman who has been recently praised. The house party, as even the smallest will, was shaking down into factions. Edward also looked relaxed. He found womanly sympathy very restful.

Ermyn noticed Angela's colour, as she lay in her deck-chair, ripening visibly, her dress pulled back to expose her chest and up to show her knees.

'You'll burn,' said Ermyn.

67

'I don't burn,' said Angela shortly, irritated by the repellent picture of peeling skin and reddened flesh that Ermyn had evoked.

'You do,' persisted Ermyn, concernedly. 'Don't you remember when you came back from Spain and you had to go to the doctor?'

'That was *Spain*, silly girl,' said Angela. 'This is *Wales*. Let's have lunch in the garden, a picnic.' She slid her sunglasses back down from her hairline to her nose and her sandals back on to her feet.

Rose made no objection. Henry hated eating out of doors, and so, she was sure, did the others. 'You are kind,' she said, as though Angela had offered to do it by herself. 'You'll find the fish in the scullery and a nice sharp knife hanging on the wall.'

Angela played this one well. 'Oh,' she cried. 'I hate cutting things' heads off. You must help me, Edward.'

'Angela's giving us a picnic,' explained Rose to the others as they gathered to look hopefully in the dining-room. They dragged the garden table out of the out-house where it was kept and carried it, cursing, to the terrace, where they had to pull it around a good deal until it ceased staggering. Michael and Henry sat down exhausted.

'Open a bottle,' said Henry. 'I hope it's well chilled.'

Edward and Angela came trotting merrily out, like runners in a relay race, with plates of fried fish. Angela had taken trouble to make it look nice, garnishing it with radishes cut to look like flowers and slices of lemon with castellated edges. It was very reminiscent of hotel food, from the thinly sliced brown bread and butter to the selection of small cheeses which Angela had gathered from the refrigerator. The plaice had the limp and glistening aspect usual to English cookery; and the midday sun, just turning its attention to the luncheon table, did not enhance its appearance.

'I can't eat this,' said Henry after a while. 'It's too hot.'

'Then I'll have it,' said Edward, scooping half-eaten fish and skin on to his plate.

'Sensible,' said Angela. 'It's wicked to waste good food.'

'I think I'll take the binoculars this afternoon and do a spot of bird watching,' said Michael.

'Well, I'm just going to rest,' said Angela, stretching her legs out languidly. 'Ready for Ursula's party.'

'Or you could hire a hack,' suggested Rose, 'and go for a nice ride.'

'Hardly,' said Angela coldly. The riding-school up the valley taught the local little girls and many of the visitors. It was absurd and outrageous that the most aristocratic of pursuits should be made available to all and sundry in this casual manner. 'I rode a lot last week at home,' she went on. 'Mother's training a young mare for one of her neighbours. She's quite amazing for her age. Once a week she teaches handicapped children to ride.' As the children were handicapped already they weren't likely to turn up in the English Show Jumping trials among their betters.

'I think that's amazing,' said Rose.

'Why are you so pale, Rose?' asked Angela. 'You look as though you hadn't been out at all. If you're afraid the sun's drying effects will give you wrinkles you only need to get a really good moisturiser.'

'Tans are common,' said Rose. 'Those deep-brown ladies have been lying around in their knickers and bras

69

reading trashy magazines and sipping iced drinks. And tanned men are on the dole, on the game, or on the run.'

'What very peculiar ideas you have,' said Angela.

'I'm going to sleep,' said Henry, making thankfully for the drawing-room.

Ermyn watched him, thinking what a pity it was that there was no war for him to excel in. He was quite wasted in peacetime in his dull civilian clothes and his dull civilian job. He would look magnificent in uniform, vermilion, gold and indigo – bring tears to the eyes dying gallantly at his post. Men were made for war. Without it they wandered greyly about, getting under the feet of the women, who were trying to organise the really important things of life. When they couldn't make war men made money – and trouble and a dreadful nuisance of themselves. Ermyn had seen Rose sigh with exasperation when Henry dusted his shoes with the kitchen cloths, and Angela had said quite openly that she couldn't *bear* to have Michael around all day . . .

'I'm going to pick bilberries,' said Ermyn, recalling herself to the moment. 'We can make a pie.'

'The visitors have trodden on all the bilberries,' said Rose. 'You'd find yourself in the foothills of Snowdon before you came across a whole one.'

'Then I shall go and pick flowers,' said Ermyn, who was afraid that if she stayed she would be expected to make conversation with Angela and Edward.

'I'll come with you,' said Rose, who feared that if she stayed she would be expected to sleep with Henry. She would really have liked to go up into the attics, but Angela would find her. She felt active and curious and well, with none of the mild hypnotic languor so essential

70

to successful sexual intercourse. The day was fine, there was a light breeze and she had drunk nothing at lunch. Again, were it not for Angela, she could have gone into her cool kitchen and made some stews and strange aromatic ice-creams. Rose liked to cook alone, safe from advice, and where no one could see what she was doing.

Ermyn looked at her, unsmiling, not quite sure that she had heard aright. 'Are you coming too?' she asked.

'Yes,' said Rose definitely, and Ermyn was relieved. She was never quite sure that Rose loved her, and signs of favour were reassuring.

'Hurry,' said Rose impatiently. Ermyn had the victimised look of a girl in a portrait -- not the beaming confident sort whose father is paying, but the sort who looks bewilderedly at the lower left-hand corner of the canvas and whom the artist means to seduce.

They carried in the plates, Ermyn imagining the walk up the mountain. When they got to the end of the lane where there was a kissing gate and the grass began she would take her shoes off. For a while the short grass clung to the mountain like a shrunken woolly; then it gave way to heather and bilberry bushes and tall ferns. On the top were rushes and small talkative streams and the breezes that followed them. Perhaps Rose would slip on a wet stone and have to be helped home, saying 'Thank God you were with me, Ermyn.'

'Do hurry,' said Rose, who was annoyed with herself. She had no desire to go for a walk with Ermyn. She had been incautious. It would have been enough to put on a big hat and some gardening gloves and take the secateurs to pretend to deadhead roses. It would have made Angela uneasy too. She swore.

71

They left Angela and Edward beginning to sink into the torpid ill-temper that comes to people who drink too much white wine out of doors on a hot day.

'It seems very unlike Rose to go wild-flowering,' said Angela. 'I hope she doesn't pull up any roots.'

*　　　*　　　*

When they had gone through the kissing gate and left behind the flies that held dominion in the lane, Rose and Ermyn stopped, as people always did, to catch their breath and look down on the house, which was briefly visible before the curve of the mountain concealed it again. Phyllis, goblin-sized, was standing in the stable yard. As they looked, Gomer came round the side of the house, and Phyllis straightened up and pointed at the kitchen door.

'Some little delicacy or other,' said Rose. 'I hope he keeps his choppers off the chocolate cake.'

She had first seen the house from here one cold December day soon after they came to Llanelys. She and her father had been out to steal holly and had gone on walking when they couldn't find any with berries. 'There'll be some down there,' her father had said. 'That's the sort of people always have berries to their holly.' Rose hadn't answered him. She had just stood in the dank mist, her hands pushed down in the pockets of her neat brown coat with the velvet collar, her eyes narrowed, watching the house tethered like a lovely goat in the gardens. She had been silent on the way home, and irritable when her father spoke to her. Rose was always able to feel for houses the emotion other people felt for animals, or even other people.

72

It was cooler on the mountain now, the sky not the vulgar true-blue of Tory party conferences or seaside postcards but a pale lemon-washed blue feathered with faint clouds.

'This is the sort of summer,' remarked Rose for something to say, 'that people think summers were always like when they were a child.'

'Yes,' agreed Ermyn, although this was not her experience. She remembered a number of cold, bad-tempered summers. When it was fine the au pairs had made her go down to the beach, where the local children teased her and the au pairs grew fractious at the extraordinary lack of young men. Most of them had only taken the job because she had two older brothers, but Henry and Michael never stayed for long and when they left the au pairs were more bored and cross than ever.

Rose wished Ermyn were more responsive: she wasn't unintelligent, but she reminded her of a class at a night-school earnestly anxious to listen and not give any trouble.

'Hurry up,' said Rose. The twins would have made her laugh by now, or frightened her hiding behind the broken-backed stone walls.

Ermyn wondered without surprise why Rose was annoyed with her, not yet realising how hateful other people could be in the absence of the beloved.

Sheep moved slowly in front of them, eating as they went. Ermyn could hear the tugging sound as they cropped the short turf. The sea was inaudible. It crept silently over the sand far below them, like a cat on small white paws. Ermyn liked the sea at a distance. She would lie awake listening to it in the equinoctial gales,

73

dangerously playful, flinging up the stones on the promenade, advancing and retreating like a kitten in a cornfield all through the dark, roaring nights. She began to dream again. When Father . . . if Father . . . She struggled to eliminate a hint of wishful thinking. The rest of the family would not be there. They would simply dematerialise – at no pain or inconvenience to themselves, of course – and she and Rose would live alone in the house. The seasons were very clear and distinct when you led a solitary life. They would make the most of winter – the tiny days, the heavy golden-skirted skies that threatened snow. They would light both fires in the drawing-room; the smoke would rush wildly up the chimneys, and then bow and scatter before the waiting winds. Rose would make toast. In the morning the snow would lie glittering on the fields under low skies of Prussian blue . . . A figure intruded into her mental image, a tall figure hatted, belted and gaitered striding along with a gun under his arm . . . Spring then, thought Ermyn. Thin, chill and watery when the rain blackened the purple slate flags and you could watch it through the drawing-room windows coming over the mountains blown sideways like a curtain. When you went out it swung at you, enveloped you in folds of bitter wetness. She remembered the twins and with faint reluctance included them, feeling that Rose would perhaps not be content without them. They would go to look for the first catkins by the stream and rejoice at the celandines. She would wrap the twins up well, wind their scarves around their small faces, tuck in their drifting, blinding hair . . .

February days the colour of seagulls when the salt-edged wind swept the sky and the sea and the houses and

74

chapels, bleaching them all to white and pastel greys . . .
Once, long ago, a gull had got its wing impaled on the
lightning conductor of the English Congregational
church. Someone had noticed it and sent for old Mr Jones
the grocer who had a gun. He shot at it and shot at it,
getting redder and madder all the time, but he couldn't
hit it, and it hung there, screeching, flying frenziedly on
the spot while a crowd gathered. Ermyn's nanny at the
time couldn't think why they didn't send for the Captain,
a dead shot. Where *she* came from they looked up to
the gentry. Ermyn couldn't remember what happened
then – whether, next time she saw the lightning conductor, it was innocent of seagull, or whether the fraying
corpse had hung there for years, or whether she had
never looked to see . . . It had been so unsuitably skittish
– the feathered flapping above the square granite
blocks. . . .

'Wait,' said Rose stopping abruptly. In the distance
someone with binoculars was spying on a hawk hovering
over an outcrop of rock. They sat down until he had
moved away and then went on.

The landscape was changing, the white wisps of bog
cotton and the leonine tufts of wind-swept marsh grass
left behind. Now there were the remains of old stone
enclosures, ruined cottages and barren lichened fruit trees.
A stunted cherry stood helplessly alone, its trunk stock-
inged in ivy. Ermyn had seen it hung with blossom like
an old woman in a girl's party dress, pale flowers iced
against the mad spring sky. Oh darling, thought Ermyn,
but could think of no reason to say it. It seemed strange
that people had once lived here, called across the stone
walls, eaten the cherries. They had left nothing of them-

75

selves. The saint was more real – the angry girl who lay in death in the cell at the end of the church . . .

When the Captain was a boy and gamekeepers were more plentiful, one had killed himself up here. First he had shot a dog, and when the farmer who owned it had asked what he thought he was doing he had shot him, and when the farmer's daughter had remonstrated he had shot her too. The Captain's father, his employees and all the men of the village had quartered the moors and searched many many miles all day and night until, coming wearily home at first light, they heard another shot. The gamekeeper had spent the night in his own cottage with his own dogs, and then he had gone out with his gun and put it to the roof of his mouth and pulled the trigger, and his cap had sailed off his head up and up into the topmost boughs of a tree, and no one could get it down again. It hung there for years. 'Damn,' said the men. 'That old tree wasn't safe, see? Fall down any minute.' Ermyn wondered which tree it was, whether any fragments of loud tweed still adhered to the rough twigs . . . like the gull on the lightning conductor. Images of death, hanging inaccessibly as far as the things of earth could reach into the sky . . .

'We're here,' said Rose.

The church stood before them, small, grey and stoical, surrounded by gravestones. Wild flowers grew in profusion. This, it was said, was because they had been watered by the blood of the saint's pet lamb. A prince from a neighbouring district had eaten it when out on an abortive hunting trip. The saint – the princess from the sea – had seen to it that he died in a dreadful manner, which the legend left unspecified. She had always been a bad-

76

tempered and spiteful girl, given to lecturing her father and his court on their profligate ways and showing no concern at all when the flood overtook them. As the years went by, according to the legend, she had never given a thought to her father's drowned bones, with the fishes floating between them and the ale mingling with the salt sea. She lay in wait for unsuspecting travellers and lectured them. After a while, so strange is the human heart, pilgrims visited her in great numbers especially to be berated, to have contumely poured upon them and to quail beneath her bitter scornful tongue. Of the lamb it was said that its bones lay concealed in the churchyard and took on flesh and wool and life every spring. For a time at Easter, Ermyn had imagined Virginia Woolf to be the incarnation; but the saint's lamb always returned to its unearthly hibernation and Virginia Woolf was still waxing fat on Rose's snapdragons. Father dismissed the whole thing as vicious rumour, perhaps because the prince had borne the same name as himself.

'I wonder what she did to him,' said Rose.

'I suppose he *was* one of us,' said Ermyn, reluctantly.

The door was open. Inside, the church was as clean and clear as a blown egg.

'It's so peaceful,' said Ermyn.

'You needn't whisper,' said Rose contemptuously. 'There's no one here.' She detested protestantism, from the pneumatic sterility of Milton to the ankle socks and hairy calves of Peggy *parchedig*, the vicar's wife. She had been given this appellation, which meant 'reverend', because the village considered her to be minimally more of a man than her husband.

'Oh,' said Ermyn. Perhaps Rose was right. The church

was very tidy; there was no sign of God. The reformers had settled here – clumsy, blind and flightless – and where was the bird? 'Poor princess,' she said. 'Poor little saint.'

'I wouldn't waste my compassion,' said Rose. 'She lived up here for years and years. She must have been tough, and from all one hears she was a shocking little bitch.'

'I hope the lamb was tough too,' said Ermyn, making a joke to ease her painful sense of pity. She closed the door quietly and laid her hands flat against the stone to reassure the sleeping saint that she was not forgotten. Ermyn knew that God's and the popular taste in people were seldom consonant.

'We'd better hurry,' said Rose, cutting scabious and tiny wild cornflowers with a pair of small steel scissors. A cloud swept swiftly over the sun and the colour drained out of everything.

On the way home Ermyn looked down at Elys Water. It cut in deeply from the sea, steep, sudden and treacherous. Traces of mad dog foam glistened on its sides and the receding tide churned angrily in it. The council had fenced it round and no one had jumped in since barbiturates became freely available, but Ermyn would never see it as merely geographical: it was distorted for ever by her childish nightmares, cutting into the calm coastline like a hare lip.

A cool mischievous wind followed them home, whisking scraps of paper and cigarette boxes across their path, blowing back the heather to reveal old tin cans and broken bottles.

*   *   *

In the house a strong smell of expensive floral scent made it apparent that Angela was getting ready for the party.

'Hurry up, you two,' she cried, running downstairs. 'It'll take us at least an hour to get there.'

'She smells as though she was *made* of flowers,' said Ermyn, 'like Blodeuwedd, the woman in the *Mabinogion* who Llew Llaw Gyffes murdered Gronw Pebyr for.'

'All sex and violets,' said Rose.

'I think it was broom and the flowers of the oak, and meadowsweet,' offered Ermyn.

'I was making a joke,' explained Rose; 'but I won't do it again, I promise.'

*   *   *

Ermyn hurried to her room and started to search in her wardrobe before she realised she'd forgotten to unpack her dress. She dragged it from her suitcase and shook it. It wasn't too creased. She combed her hair and wiped her face with the corner of her sheet – there was no time to wash.

'I'm not coming,' said Rose.

'It'll seem strange if you don't,' said Angela severely. She looked as though she was dressed to go to a wedding at a superior hotel: not over-festive no hat or carnation; a distant cousin of the groom perhaps. Her frock was light and patterned in white and black and orange and green; it floated about her knees and plunged discreetly between her breasts. She had put on bright lipstick and a little eye shadow. Her conception of smartness had been formed in an earlier decade and was confined to her class and age group.

'How lovely you look,' said Rose.

'Why aren't you coming?' asked Angela. 'Phyllis will be with Father.'

'I don't want to,' said Rose. 'I am in search neither of sexual adventure nor of social contact and I wouldn't go all that way for Ursula's cup.' She remembered previous evenings shivering in the wind from the straits, her heels sunk into the soft lawn. She only enjoyed parties where people asked her what she did, so that she could reply that she was an ordinary housewife and watch them wondering who it could be they had offended. At Ursula's parties people asked if you were going to the next party or had been recently to the theatre.

'If you want interesting conversation at Ursula's you have to take one of your own friends with whom to have it – like a bottle party.' She waved her hand. 'Take Edward. He can talk to the marquess for a treat.' Edward was very fond of people with titles. They sent him Christmas cards with personal greetings, which he then quoted in his column.

'Of course Edward's coming,' said Angela, glad that Rose wasn't and at the same time annoyed by what she considered to be affectation – it was ridiculous for someone like Rose to pretend she didn't want to go to a party with a marquess.

'I'll stay with you,' said Henry.

'No. You go,' said Rose.

'All right,' he said equably.

'We can take my car,' said Michael. 'You girls can go in the back with Henry, and Edward can come in front and get a good view of the viaduct and the bay.'

Angela was put out at this.

'I wish Rose was coming,' said Ermyn with maddening naïveté. 'She's so much prettier than anyone else.' She glanced back at Rose in the late afternoon light. Rose's jawbone was as light and taut as the shaft of a quill feather and her eyes gleamed like sea-wrack flames. How cool she looked, thought Ermyn humbly, trying to ease her dress a little away from her own damp flesh. Rose had the iron invincibility of the beloved, the kind of self-assurance usually found only in those philosophers or scientists whose disciplines do not permit of doubt.

'Oh come,' said Angela. 'Serena and Belinda will be there, you know.'

Edward came out, and she regarded him critically. He looked odd, but he was a distinguished journalist and could pass on the grounds of eccentricity – for which quality Angela had the usual English reverence.

Rose watched his retreating back with dislike. His clothes were clean but he had an unloved look. His shirt had been savagely, professionally, laundered and there was a small vertical rent on each side of his tie. His wife refused to do housework, crying with alcoholic fervour that after her academic career – and she could have done anything, *anything* d'ye hear – she wasn't going to let her brain deteriorate into bashed neeps doing his sodding washing. So he looked as though he might be found behind the counter of a back-street tobacconist's in an area scheduled for urban redevelopment. The abjectness of his poverty mystified his friends. 'We're none of us as well-off as we were,' they said. 'This government . . .' But even the Inland Revenue could hardly be blamed for his apparent penury. In the end they casually shrugged and supposed it must be his drinks bill.

81

Edward went off eagerly like a dog on a walk.

Jack the Liar and Phyllis were talking together softly in the kitchen. They stopped when Rose came in, and Phyllis began to wipe the table with a damp cloth.

'I'll be off then now,' said Jack. 'See you in the morning.'

'See Gomer gets his supper,' said Phyllis. Casually she passed him a paper bag bulging with hidden foodstuffs.

*   *   *

Rose went up to the attic. It was hot and dusty just under the roof and she took off her dress. Occasionally something squeaked in the rafters, and to be on the safe side she took an old deerstalker hat from the top of a brass-bound trunk and set it on her head. A dimmed cheval-glass caught her reflection and she frowned at the curious creature who crouched in her place frowning. The stairs groaned and she turned.

'Gomer?' she said.

The stairs creaked again, but there was no reply. She went down and locked the attic door. 'You are ill at ease tonight,' she said to the house, as she began her investigations. She had reached the Captain's wife's things, stacked neatly together, packed away in trunks and suitcases. Even her books were here in cardboard boxes – D. H. Lawrence and Dorothy Richardson; Proust, Joyce and Ronald Firbank; an early work of psychology: Rose glanced through it, her eyebrows raised.

When she grew bored she took up a tube of glue and began to mend an old Noah's Ark with all its little people and animals. There was nothing she liked better than to

82

have the ordering of things great and small, animate and inanimate.

*   *   *

Ermyn stood shivering at the edge of the Watcyn Hogge lawn. Henry had met a valued old friend, and Michael had sidled away from her through a dense crowd of chattering gentlefolk; he was ashamed of her. She had spoken to one or two of Father's old friends and was quite sure Father would not have been proud of her either. In the past she had heard people saying in low admiring tones that the Captain was a dreadful dog but so marvellous with women that even when it was all over they never bore him any ill-will. For a time she had imagined that possibly he blamed her for the death of his heart's beloved, and that that was why he seemed so distant; but as she grew older she gathered that this wasn't so. Father believed that to deserve a place in the human race women should be pretty and bold – warm, available and golden-hearted. Ermyn herself made no effort to please and seemed unaware that that was what she was for. Things that cringed were not attractive; they made Father mad. Ermyn could see him now, quivering with anger like a mongoose, spluttering, his eyes bulging. In a really awful temper Father always reminded her of an enraged baby – six-feet-four and sixteen stone – absurd and indescribably terrifying.

Ermyn wiped coldly sweating hands on the Indian cotton kaftan that had seemed so charming in the London street market when her aunt had urged her to buy it. There were some people of her own age in the crowd –

slender, androgynous, cosmopolitan, glossily pale and jewelled. They were unsmiling, and listlessly assured, and even more alarming than the group of indigenous youth who had formed a little party of their own away from the rest. These tumbled together boisterously, but a little resentfully, giving the impression that while they were eager for sexual experience it was not with each other. The girls wore strapless evening frocks and stoles and dated local hairstyles, and were all overweight, having come recently from boarding-school meals and the hockey pitch. They had always despised Ermyn for being only a day girl, although, as she had explained time and again, it was not that Father couldn't afford the fees but that as her home was so near it would have been silly to board. 'My father likes me with him,' she had told them.

'Oh hullo, Ermyn,' said a large girl in dingy white, a dying orchid on her large bosom. Her dress might well have been a gym slip and the orchid her house badge. It was the colour of dried blood and to Ermyn's eyes had a slightly guilty, defiant look. 'What are you doing here? Are you going on to the dance?' She obviously thought it unlikely.

'No,' said Ermyn. 'My father's ill.'

'Why are you here then?' asked someone else, and giggled.

'Because I am,' said Ermyn bitterly, wondering how long it had to be before time came between her and such taunts.

'Who is your father?' asked a big fattish boy, velvet-suited and babyishly pink. His ruffled shirt might have been a christening gown, and she thought she could remember him at a children's party when they were very

84

young, with bits of banana sandwich stuck to his plump cheeks. This gave Ermyn confidence and she told him her name, clearly.

'Oh,' said the boy, a little dashed and looking aside.

The hunting instinct was very strong in these people. Had they not recognised her by her name as one of their own species they would have pursued her, baying, down to the water's edge and there demolished her, snuffling, grunting and tearing. They would have howled with satiated glee and flung around her ragged, bloodied remnants, like the hounds with a hare . . . Her eyes widened.

'Well, I want something to eat,' said a dark girl in electric blue, bored with the dulling presence of this newcomer. 'Where's the little man with the goodies?'

Ermyn walked away. A ruddy-faced squire – sleek and healthy, although already quite drunk – came unseeingly towards her. He smiled meaninglessly and Ermyn knew that if she hadn't moved he would have walked right over her. 'Reggie . . .' he cried. 'Now look, old . . .' He disappeared in the crowd.

Someone was telling a story about the only house left in England where you could get a right and a left in butlers. There were peals, guffaws and modified shrieks of laughter, but it sounded to Ermyn as though a dreadful accident had taken place. The narrator was famous for his wit and his anecdotes, but Rose said that the upper classes had low standards and were easily pleased, and that he'd never have made it on the Halls.

Ermyn moved on, unamused and tentatively disapproving. Rather than waste the time, she would think about Father, practise methods of helping him, endeavour to approach his uncertain spirit and encourage it. She backed into the rhododendrons and went down to the edge of the straits. The fool's gold of the sunset, shattered into weightless coins, lay on the shifting leaden grey of the sea. Father never spoke of it, but he put great store by money – it was a measure of virtue and responsibility: people who were disrespectful of the power of money, like nuns, or careless of its ownership like thieves, or who thought it grew on trees like the working class, were mad or bad or both and deserved to be put away. The tide was turning and the wind had ripped the sunset sky into glorious rags of crimson and gold and green, a martial banner at the height of the battle. Father's spirit should be here striding out in the great surge of wind and water, the shade of one of his little terriers rocking along at his side . . . On the other hand, conceded Ermyn unhappily, his spirit would probably rather be up on the lawn with a stiff gin and one of the highly seasoned blondes he always preferred. This was an area where she felt incompetent to help. She wandered slowly back to look for Angela.

'Oh terrible,' Angela was saying '. . . it's sheer envy. They can't bear to see anyone in the least better off than themselves.' She indicated vaguely the vast pile towering behind them in its acres of gardens. 'What would this place be without Ursula living in it? A mere museum.'

'Some of them are awfully sweet, though,' said her companion. 'We open our place on Sundays all through the summer, and one little boy said to his mother, "Oh mummy, it's just like God's house." '

'Sweet,' said Angela, and they laughed a little together.

'Oh hullo, Ermyn,' said Angela. 'Are you being good?' She didn't introduce her.

Awkwardly, Ermyn began to wander off again. 'Do you know what I mean by *fey*?' she heard. 'I always call . . .'

She made her way around groups of people who smiled at her forbiddingly and held their glasses high so that she shouldn't spill them. The women were mostly dressed in imitation of royalty. They wore light matching coats over their frocks and clutched their handbags awkwardly, sticking their bottoms out a little and standing with their ugly comfortable shoes apart. Once an empress of China had been born with crippled feet, and all the other women had bound their own to simulate or mitigate her deformity . . . Ermyn was thankful to see Edward standing alone on the terrace leaning against a heavily ornamented iron urn containing a topiarised bay tree.

As she approached, Edward turned his head and was sick in it. He then walked round it and began to make certain other unmistakable preparations.

On her right her godmother was walking slowly towards her along the terrace talking seriously to the bishop and his wife. Ermyn stepped in front of them.

'Hullo,' she said.

'Hullo, er . . .' said the bishop smiling his professional smile. Rose said they were all given the secret of it when they were ordained. She had seen black bishops with that same smile pasted on their dusky chops. They would have looked more natural and dignified, she said, with shreds of missionary adhering to their marvellous teeth . . .

'Hullo, dear,' said Lady Watcyn Hogge, mildly surprised. 'You remember Ermyn,' she told the bishop. 'The Captain's daughter.'

'Of course, of course,' said the bishop heartily. 'How is the dear man?' he added in more ecclesiastical tones.

'Very ill,' said Ermyn. 'Dying.'

'Dear me,' said someone, rather shocked at these unfestive words.

Ermyn searched her brain for a topic of conversation. She didn't dare turn round to see if Edward had gone, in case their eyes followed hers.

Although his diocese was over the border, the bishop had preached to the school several times – his wife was the sister of her headmistress. Ermyn knew what he liked, if she could only remember. He thought that Jesus had had a 'tremendous sense of fun' and been an astute politician. Or had he been speaking about himself? Otherwise all she could remember was that he seemed to believe that a Christian pastor's chief duty lay in seeing that his parishioners had enough coal and were not unduly troubled by aircraft noise.

'Ecumenism,' she said. 'I wanted to ask what you thought about it?'

'That's a good subject,' said the bishop amiably. He rather prided himself on his way with lunatics.

But Ermyn had forgotten what it meant. 'That is,' she said carefully, beginning again, 'I wanted to ask you – how do you set about persuading young people, that is people *my* age, to go to church?'

They were looking at her very oddly, but Ermyn was used to that. She waited for an answer.

'Well,' said the bishop, speaking in the strangulated patrician tones peculiar to the Established Church. 'That's a large subject.'

'I think,' said his wife, 'that what really brings them in is a really *smashing* liturgy.'

'Yes,' said the bishop, resigning himself to the edification of this odd girl. 'My wife is right. And, you know, we were the very first to have a beat group playing in our cathedral.'

'Gosh,' said Ermyn.

'It's quite logical, you know,' continued his wife. 'All hymn tunes were contemporary music in their day.'

'Crumbs,' said Ermyn. The compulsion to turn round was almost undeniable. She stared at the bishop's wife until her eyes began to water.

'I'll leave you to your little chat,' said Lady Watcyn Hogge moving, to Ermyn's great relief, back the way she had come.

The bishop went with her, but the bishop's wife had hit her stride. Taking Ermyn's arm, she led her to an elaborate stone bench, where they sat down. 'You see, my dear . . .' she said, and Ermyn learnt in the intervals, when she could prevent her attention from straying, that while the bishop's wife could see no theological arguments against lady priests, in her own view it was her husband's duty to deal directly with God, while she best served her Lord by being a good wife and mother. 'It may seem a little unfair,' she said. 'Being married to Hugh means I have very little time for my own interests, but then Christianity is not about justice but *love*.'

'Oh, thanks frightfully,' said Ermyn. 'I do see.' She remembered Rose standing in the scoured church and reflected that the bishop's wife would make her sick. At once she grew hot with shame at her ingratitude. It was very kind of this nice woman to talk to her for such a long time when there were so many interesting people around. She smiled widely and began to rise, but the bishop's wife restrained her.

'Hugh always says . . .' she went on inexorably, 'that to praise the Lord is a *joyous* thing. He says that it is natural to cheer when your team wins and it is just as natural to cheer on hearing the good news of the Gospel. Although, of course,' she went on, 'Christianity is also about suffering. Jesus on the cross . . .' She gazed sorrowfully at the jumble of humanity scoffing laden biscuits on the pampered lawns.

'Yes, thanks awfully,' said Ermyn, growing a little distraught. 'I must find . . .'

Angela came up, looking aggrieved. 'Oh, there you are, Ermyn.' She was really looking for Edward.

'The bishop's wife,' said Ermyn, indicating her politely as she backed away.

'Oh,' said Angela, mollified. 'How do you do.' They began to talk.

Ermyn found the car and crawled inside, feeling cold and very tired, but when they were all ready to go there was no sign of Edward.

'We can't just leave him,' cried Angela.

'He'll find his way back. He always does,' said Henry. Edward had the uncanny ability of the chronically drunk, not merely to survive, but to get himself taken care of.

Angela didn't like the idea of abandoning him, but there was nothing she could do short of instituting a search and she found she was reluctant to do this. Something told her it would not be wise.

'Goodbye, dear,' said Lady Watcyn Hogge. 'I'm so sorry about the Captain.'

Angela smiled deprecatingly, gratefully.

Cries of farewell and the noises of departure echoed about them.

'Good party,' said Henry, as they got into the car. 'Enjoy yourself, Ermyn?'

'Yes, thank you,' said Ermyn. 'I met some girls from school. They were going on to a dance. They asked me to go with them, but I said I couldn't.'

'The Season, I suppose,' said Angela. 'Mummy always says it's absurdly ostentatious to keep it up in this day and age.'

'Mother just caught the last year of three feathers and a train,' remarked Michael.

'There was some real *point* to it in those days,' said Angela.

Season, thought Ermyn. Bitch in season, oysters in season. Rabbits were always in season. Inglorious game; game for anything; fair game. Poor herbivores – they had no time for games: their only chance of survival lay underground, or in constant flight, or in unremitting reproduction. They must be so tired by now, all the rabbits . . .

'Do wake up, Ermyn. You're lying on my arm and it's gone dead.'

* * *

In the attic Rose lifted her head as she heard the car whining up the lane. Unhurriedly she put on her frock, picked up a photograph album, turned out the light, locked the door and went downstairs.

'Edward?' she asked, as they trooped in, flushed with cup and society.

91

'I'll leave a door open for him,' said Henry.

'No you won't,' said Rose. 'Visitors keep calling to ask if we do bed and breakfast. You could find yourself sharing a bed with Mum and Dad and little Gary and Sharon. He can sleep in the stable.'

'I'll hear him,' said Angela. 'I'm a very light sleeper. You really should have come, Rose. It was absolute blissikins.'

As it was Friday, there was only lentil soup and bread and cheese for supper: very good lentil soup and very good cheese since Rose much preferred to honour the letter of the old law, rather than submit herself to the vague dispensations and ill-defined freedoms of the spirit of Vatican II.

* * *

Next morning Edward was discovered asleep behind a settle in the dining-room. He had been sick again and had wrapped himself in an irreplaceable linen tablecloth.

'Your friend,' said Phyllis grimly, passing through with a shovelful of ashes.

'No friend of mine,' said Rose. 'He probably ate something he found in the garden.'

'He won't meet his deadline if he goes on like this,' said Angela, knowledgeable and concerned.

'He doesn't drink when he's working,' said Henry.

'Then I do wish you'd give him something to do,' said Rose, hopping a little.

'Poor Edward,' mourned Angela, leaning round the settle and brushing a strand of hair from his forehead. 'He has so much on his mind.'

'He seems to have had quite a bit on his stomach,' said Rose.

'You don't understand,' said Angela smugly. 'He's been telling me all about himself. He's an extraordinary vulnerable and sensitive person and he feels things very deeply.'

Ermyn watched from the dining-room door. 'He's awful,' she said involuntarily.

'Don't be so silly, Ermyn,' said Angela. 'It really is time you grew up a bit. Go and put the kettle on and I'll make him some black coffee and toast.'

'You didn't see what he was doing,' muttered Ermyn, surprisingly uncowed. She wished she'd let the bishop fall over him – let Ursula look in the urn and see what he'd done.

'I expect he was just washing his hands in the shrubbery, or something,' said Angela. 'Men always do.'

Henry got a bottle of whisky from the sideboard and poured half a tumblerful. 'This'll put him right,' he said.

A short time later Edward had stopped shuddering and gasping. He sat on the terrace perfectly composed and rational, telling Angela about his walking tour in New Mexico gathering material for his next book.

Angela listened with interest and concentration. 'As a family,' she told him, 'we're all tremendous walkers. You see so much more of the countryside, don't you?'

After a while she brought him a singed kipper and some nicely cut brown bread and butter, and he ate it.

*   *   *

Ermyn carried a copy of *Country Life* up to her bedroom.

She took her school bible from the bookshelf and folded it in the magazine. She had promised herself that she would never sit by daylight reading in her bedroom ever again. She went through the dining-room and into the long parlour. It was seldom used and smelled of old cold wood-ash and damp. She sat down in a chintz-covered arm chair and began to read, starting at Genesis, determined to be tidy and methodical, and keeping *Country Life* ready in case someone should come in and ask what she was doing – she felt they would consider Bible-reading not merely aberrant behaviour, but very poor form.

Blod, the woman who did the rough, cycled slowly across the yard surprising Ermyn, who hadn't realised she was looking out of the window. Blod's knees were the size and shape of babies' heads. Faceless twins, they appeared rhythmically in turn, repellent and pitiful. She was going to kneel on them, thought Ermyn, while she polished the flags. She hid her bible under a cushion and got up. The window was flawed; the yard quivered and doubled until she moved to the next window. 'It is time for coffee,' she said deliberately, silently taking control.

As she had expected, Rose was staging elevenses. The coffee was percolating and there were plain biscuits in a wide blue-rimmed jar. The sight filled Ermyn with sorrow. Too late, she thought. It came too late. She had been brought up untidily, inured to disorder: it would be affectation for her now to live comfortably – would take a degree of pretence she felt herself incapable of. The theatricality of Rose's housekeeping made all too obvious the deficiencies of her own upbringing. She knew it was foolish and irrational, but she felt inferior and longed ungratefully for instant coffee in an unwashed mug. The feeling did not lessen her love for Rose. She knew Rose was pretending, but Rose did it so well. Disloyalty, said Ermyn to herself, wondering where her loyalties lay. She wished it was permitted to choose.

'Rose,' she said suddenly.

'Mm?' said Rose.

Ermyn brought out her idea for the very first time and exposed it to the warm coffee-laden air of the kitchen.

'How do you become a Roman Catholic?'

'You don't,' said Rose without hesitation.

Ermyn was unrebuffed. Like a drunk, she persisted. 'No, *how*?'

'Nobody does any more,' said Rose.

'They must,' said Ermyn. 'They *must*.'

Loyalty, coffee, and the concept of home surged dream-like in her mind. She sat down and took a biscuit, revising her idea.

'I was talking to the bishop,' she said.

Rose wasn't listening. 'You'd never get in,' she said, 'past the people falling over themselves to get out.'

'Oh why?' asked Ermyn, leaden and hopeless. Since her day as a bridesmaid she had thought of the Church as a last resort, a final sure goal, to be taken when all else failed.

'Coffee?' asked Rose.

'Yes please,' said Ermyn.

Blod was filling her bucket in the scullery. 'Terrible thing about your *da*,' she called cheerfully.

'Terrible,' Ermyn agreed in a loud voice.

'They modernised it,' said Rose, taking up the thread. 'They fell victim to the municipal line of thought which goes: "That's beautiful. It must be old. We'd better knock it down."'

'Yes, I know,' said Ermyn, thinking of the building site in the fields below. 'Don't you go to church any more?'

'No,' said Rose, 'I don't. Certainly not.'

Ermyn now felt steady and strong. She almost felt sorry for Rose.

But Rose went on. 'They want you to kiss the person next to you,' she said. 'We've already got Moody and Sankey, and soon it'll be snake-handling.'

In the face of such wicked assurance Ermyn was lost again. 'Love,' she suggested uncertainly.

'Yuk,' said Rose.

Ermyn flushed. 'You're beautiful,' she said, with reproach.

Rose knew that perfectly well. 'At the consecration,' she said dreamily, 'they do a sort of advertiser's announcement. You think for a moment they're telling you God's blood is untouched by human hand, a sort of guarantee of wholesomeness – though I'd always been led to believe it was feet. But they're actually explaining it is *made* by human hands. They're very honest, you see. They don't want to feel they're putting anything over on anybody. I think it's meant for the enlightenment of the credulous, who previously thought it came straight from Heaven in vast ethereal tankers. And they're creeping up on transubstantiation, circling it with a net. It'll be the next to go, and then heigh ho for the gates of Hell.'

There was that note of satisfaction again. Ermyn now identified it correctly. Rose was not a philanthropist.

Ermyn thought with regret of Rose's wedding day: incense on the arctic air, tiny tiered candle flames sway-

ing in the draughts, the sanctuary lamp flowering san-
guinely. Looking back, Ermyn saw Rose fitted into her
wedding day like a new doll in its box, paper and
ribbons undisturbed. A carefully looked-after doll might
stay beautiful, but it was never so much itself as when it
stood newly in its box. Ermyn had been very grave and
well-conducted that day. The family, who had slipped
effortlessly into the comfortable modernity of atheism,
which fitted them better than the best clothes of Angli-
canism, had nevertheless retained a latent mistrust of
popery and fidgeted a little and raised their eyebrows.
Younger or less well-bred, they would have nudged,
giggled and snorted. But Ermyn had been serious. They
had grown irritated with her for her careful way, her unsmiling face.

In the church garden frozen chrysanthemums had
clashed icily together in the November wind.

'The P.P. comes in from time to time to rebuke me,
but I take no notice,' said Rose complacently. 'I tell him I
stand exactly where I always stood, while the Church
has ebbed from me. I tell him I was a true, obedient
daughter of the Church but this is beyond a joke and I
will not make a fool of myself because fools decree it
should be so. Or words to that effect, you understand.'

It wasn't that Rose wouldn't suffer fools gladly: she
couldn't stand them at any price. She scowled. 'The last
time I went to Mass – and it *was* the last time – there
was the P.P. facing the congregation, standing behind his
table and joining in the singing of the negro spirituals
and the pop songs and Shall-we-gather-at-the-river. There
has always been a hint of catering about the Mass, but
previously the priest had the dignity of a master chef

97

busying himself with his *specialité*. Now he seems like a singing waiter in charge of an inadequate buffet. One is tempted to stroll up and ask for a double martini and enquire who on earth forgot to put the doings on the canapés. I wonder why they didn't keep the real Mass for me and just bring in this one for the kiddies and the mentally subnormal?'

Ermyn was nervous of the parish priest. He was a dour man, unsmiling and abstracted, with none of the merry charm that so frequently disfigures the Catholic clergy in the colder countries. She thought Rose brave, but wondered whether she was good: she was pure, but so were some poisons in that unadulterated sense. Ermyn still thought of goodness as being kind to animals, brushing your teeth night and morning, and helping.

'To do him justice,' said Rose, 'he does still dress in the proper fashion. He hasn't taken to going round in jeans and a T-shirt and a little cross on a chain round his neck imploring people to call him Roger, and he hasn't left the church to marry and devote his life to rewriting theology to conform with his own lusts and itches, and drivel on about the self-transcending nature of sex, like all those treacherous lecherous jesuits mad with the radiant freedoms of contemporary thought. But it isn't enough. Now the Church has lost its head, priests feel free to say what they think themselves, and they don't have any thoughts at all except for some rubbish about the brotherhood of man. They seem to regard Our Lord as a sort of beaten egg to bind us all together.'

She began to make a mayonnaise, requesting the Holy Souls not to let it curdle. 'It is as though,' she went on, 'one's revered, dignified and darling old mother had

98

slapped on a mini-skirt and fishnet tights and started ogling strangers. A kind of menopausal madness, a sudden yearning to be attractive to all. It is tragic and hilarious and awfully embarrassing. And of course, those who knew her before feel a great sense of betrayal and can't bring themselves to go and see her any more. Angela will be behaving like that in a few years,' she added, pouring a little wine vinegar into the bowl. 'I can see the signs already.'

Ermyn knew about treacherous deserting mothers, so she wasn't surprised. Nor was she quite prepared to give up. For the moment she put her idea away. It was a little chilled and sullied by its first reception, but by no means dead, and Ermyn had long been aware that she was not the sort of person people were always overjoyed to see and welcome. 'Can I help?' she asked.

'Not really,' said Rose. 'As it's the match tomorrow, I'm making a special dinner for tonight. They are all so fond of a little ceremony.' She didn't even attempt to make this sound like the truth but carried on pouring oil and murmuring.

Ermyn wondered what Rose was up to. She knew – had always known in an unclear, unformulated way – that Rose was playing a constant elaborate game with rules known only to herself and probably infinitely mutable. 'I could do the potatoes,' she said.

'As long as you don't gouge or scratch,' said Rose, surreptitiously sliding another egg yolk into the bowl. While there were many ways of killing a cat, the easiest was to choke it to death with cream: it involved no coercion, no show of force, and even looked like kindness.

Ermyn pushed open the wire-meshed door of the larder

and stepped forward. It was dark, and her cheek touched something damp, solid and lifeless hanging from the low ceiling. She gasped and fell back, hitting her hip on a shelf and rattling a bowl of cherries marinading glossily in brandy.

'Put the light on,' said Rose.

Ermyn regarded the huge purplish leg of mutton swaying slowly back and forth, dripping on to a dish, and thought of Father. It was death that made flesh meat, and Father wasn't dead; but the memory of all those furred and feathered creatures hanging, dull-eyed, upside down, in whom Father himself had wrought this metamorphosis, troubled her. Somewhere in the reflection was an unseemly element of triumph.

'I bumped into the meat,' she said.

'I hope it's not going off,' said Rose.

Ermyn carried the potatoes out carefully, wishing she hadn't gone in to the larder. It smelt of bananas and butter and blood, of fruit and death and darkness. When Phyllis's husband had died, the weather had been hot and Phyllis had prepared tea too early: yellow globules of butter sinking into the bread, greasy thickly cut slabs of ham, chunks of wet fruitcake, and sweet dark-brown tea – the sun shining mercilessly on it. Phyllis had put two glasses of British port on the coffin, handed them to Gomer and Jack, and watched while they drank it. Rose had been enthralled – could hardly wait for the service to end. 'Did you see that?' she kept saying. 'Did you see? The *cwpan y meirw*, the cup of death. Some loony aborigines and the Welsh are the only people who ever did that, and the aborigines have stopped. Some of them,' she said, 'thought they were ingesting the good qualities of the corpse and some that they were relieving it of its sins. The Welsh used to hire an untouchable to do it,' she explained.

Ermyn made a wry face. Death bread, dead breath. Funeral food should be light and hot and bitter in the mouth, or perhaps it was possible to exist only on splinters of ice. No one had ever tried . . .

Rose poured thick cream into the pudding. Evidence of ill-will lay openly, but unrecognisably, on the table: numerous egg shells, orange peel, chocolate wrappers, heavy cream, oil and butter and sherry, three ducks thawing flaccidly on a charger in a cold pink pool of blood. She had decided quite gratuitously that this year the home team should not win.

'What are we having?' asked Ermyn, to be polite.

'Nothing much,' said Rose. 'Egg mayonnaise and duck and stuff.'

Ermyn swallowed. 'How lovely,' she said. 'We don't have things like that in London.'

'I know,' said Rose. Ermyn, while she struggled through a secretarial course at a smart establishment, was staying with cousins of her mother's, who were thoroughly tainted with that artistic quality which the Captain had so disliked in his wife and ate Mediterranean vegetables and rice with nuts and raisins in it.

Rose was still not altogether without compassion. Having judged the calorific content and general unwholesomeness of this meal to be possibly beyond computation, she spoke. 'Don't eat too much,' she said.

Ermyn looked at her doubtfully. Rose's ears were pointed and so were her teeth. Once she had cooked din--ner for a Midlands client of Henry's who wanted to buy

101

a small valley with some fishing and shooting. She had given him prawn cocktail, steak and pretty little chips, and an antipodean thing called a pavlova – the sort of meal the family described as 'Uxbridge Country Club'. Ermyn had seen the joke, but she hadn't enjoyed the meal. He was a nice man and appreciative, and had left happily, sure he had had a splendid evening.

And there was the time soon after the wedding when Cousin Teddy, who was a Doctor of Divinity, had travelled down to see the newlyweds, and perhaps offer them his blessing, and had come off his moped at the lowest turn of the pass. Happily, the nearest hospital was well used to head injuries, being situated in the heart of mountaineering country, and Teddy had survived. Rose had taken Ermyn to see him quite frequently. She had been kind, always remembering a little present – flowers, new laid eggs, or a napkin of welsh cakes . . . New laid eggs: often at tea-time, Rose had gone into the nurses' kitchen and had herself boiled him an egg – always boiled, never poached or scrambled. The trouble was that Teddy's head had been wrapped in a swathe of tight white bandage, and Ermyn had found something disturbing in the sight of him, white-domed, beating away with his steel teaspoon, slowly and uncertainly at the white dome of the egg.

*　　　*　　　*

Blod came down to empty her bucket. 'Captain looks awful,' she said, going down the steps to the scullery.

'Well, he isn't well,' said Rose.

Angela followed, hurrying, lined with indignation. 'That woman's just bundled all the clothes I put out to

102

straighten back into my suitcase.' Angela's skirts had pronounced pleats and knife-edge creases.

'She's potty,' said Rose.

'You think everyone's potty, Rose,' said Angela impatiently. 'You know what they say about people who think that, don't you?'

'She *is* potty,' said Rose. 'She tried to borrow Phyllis's teeth to go on an outing to Rhyl. She said she knew they'd fit because they take the same size shoes.'

Angela was amused. 'I don't think that's potty. I think it's rather sweet.'

'She looks awfully old to be working so hard,' said Ermyn, blushing again as she heard the implied rebuke.

'They all look old,' said Rose. 'I keep thinking the girls I was at school with are their mothers. It annoys them no end.'

'Oh, you're so silly, Rose,' said Angela. 'Shall I start lunch?'

'It's ready,' said Rose, who had put salad and cheese and home-made bread in the dining-room, wholesome and reassuring.

Edward ate voraciously, even the rind of the cheese, and he gathered up some large crumbs with a blob of butter on the end of his knife and put them in his mouth.

'I had a letter from my mother,' said Angela. 'The children did their play. *Oedipus* in rhyming couplets.'

'Goodness,' said Rose austerely.

'Matthew's being awfully brave,' said Angela. 'His cat died of kidney failure just before we came away and I had to ring the school and tell him. He took it marvellously well. An example to us all.'

'Perhaps he didn't like it much?' suggested Rose.

103

'He adored it,' said Angela. '*Adored* it.'

'Weather looks all right for the match,' said Michael, gazing out at the sky. 'I hope it holds.'

'I'm not going to bother with it next year,' said Henry idly, stroking Rose's arm as she went past. 'There won't be any point.'

Michael was astonished. Henry's few years' seniority gave him no such powers of life and death. 'Oh, come,' he said, sitting up.

'No, really,' said Henry. 'I've had to leave Jack to get the opposition together.'

'Still,' said Michael.

'It'll be a farce,' said Henry, leaning back in his chair and gazing after Rose. 'Coffee?' he asked.

'Coming,' said Rose.

'We must keep it up,' insisted Michael.

'Edward could write an article about it,' said Angela. 'Village cricket. Pass the salt please, Ermyn. Ermyn, please pass the salt.'

'Sorry,' said Ermyn. 'I wasn't listening.' She was thinking about the pillars that held up the year – Christmas and Easter and birthdays and the 4th of June and the 12th of August, and time sagging between them, and the annual event a diminishing pillar.

In the days just after the war when the Captain had given the Elysian Field to the village in a fit of grateful generosity and instituted the annual match against the visitors, Llanelys had still been smart. Racy cotton-brokers and sober merchants had brought their families for the summer. Academics in shorts had made it their base for hiking, and among the Captain's opponents had been a few as well-born as himself. But, gradually at first,

104

and then with alarming speed, the people had taken over Llanelys and made it their own. Uncouth accents echoed on the wide sea shore, and the sand, ridged like buckled linoleum, felt the naked tread of inferior feet. The Grand Hotel had struggled to accommodate itself to the new demands, added an American bar, offered Bingo evenings, but had finally gone under and was now merely a collection of holiday flatlets. The other large hotel had become a Christian Temperance hostel and the superior boarding houses and rented villas had disappeared. The Captain had given up playing when it became clear that there were no longer any opponents worthy of him, but he liked his sons and his household to carry on the tradition. It would have been too cold a reminder of the power of time to stop it completely.

'Jack's been canvassing in the pubs,' said Henry.

They all knew what he meant. Even with the democratisation of Llanelys the pubs fell into distinct categories, Two had retained their pretensions to propriety, with stuffed fish in glass cases, framed recommendations from George Borrow, orotund descriptions of the scenery from Dr Johnson, and leathery lounges for morning coffee. The visitors who patronised these two were older, more conservative and, on the whole, family people – middle-grade civil servants, or skilled car-workers, cleanly shirted and trousered, resting from their banausic labours, stiff with the ineffable self-righteousness of the trades unionist; their wives were scented and fat, but contained. They brought an aura of home with them, of melodious chimes and tradescantia in hanging baskets, well-trained pets and immaculate lavatories. They were a joke, of course, but respectful enough and even biddable. The habitués

of the other six were a different matter – naughty, antino-
mian and wild: given to spreading litter and demanding
their rights. They lived on inflated wages or national
assistance and made unpleasant scenes on the narrow
country roads, refusing to back into the passing places.
They were funny but humourless: they didn't see themselves as others saw them. Like bad actors, they neglected
their cues, made up their own lines, and wouldn't conform. Jack frequented the six, together with the salmon-
poacher and the sheep-stealer.

'It'll be fun. It always is,' said Angela.

'I don't know why you say that,' said Rose. 'It isn't
true.'

Henry stretched lazily, straining the back of his chair.
'They're never any good,' he said, 'and they always want
to win.'

'It's a game,' said Michael.

'You all want to win too,' said Rose. 'I can't think why
you bother to deny it.'

'I love it,' said Angela. 'I won't hear a word against my
lovely Midlanders.'

'Angela knows these people,' Michael explained to
Edward. 'She went to school round there. You'd be surprised how beautiful some of the country is.'

Edward needed no explanations. He believed, as did the
family, that some people had finer-textured flesh and
purer blood, and were organically, morally better – better
in every way – than the rest; and Angela seemed to him
an entirely estimable human being – an Englishwoman.

Encouraged by his silent, obvious approval Angela continued. 'Actually, I love people like that. We had a street
carnival just before we came away. Whelk and winkle

106

stalls and a pop group, and everyone joined in. My mother was staying with us and she sat on the steps eating jellied eels. I think it's marvellous how class distinctions have completely gone.'

Angela laughed and laughed at the memory of her mother sitting there, her fingers slippery with jellied eels. 'But then,' she added more soberly, 'the children thought they'd have a jumble sale and raise some money for the N.S.P.C.C. They painted a poster – it was awfully good – and hung it on the railings. They got all their old clothes and some toys and put them on a table in front of the house. I had to retrieve a few, of course – Matthew's fairisle sweater and Louise's school shoes.' She laughed indulgently. 'It's a marvellous way of tidying the house, and I do think it's awfully good for them to realise there are children not as fortunate as themselves. It gives them a sense of the wider world.'

'If there were more parents like you,' said Edward, through a mouthful of the cherries Rose had put on the table to see how many he would eat, 'the country wouldn't be in its present state.'

'I do agree,' said Angela. 'Government hand-outs can never be the same as simple generosity.'

'I'll clear the table,' said Ermyn.

'No, sit down,' said Rose. 'I've got something to show you.'

She got up, easily, silkily, without jarring the chair. From the dresser cupboard she drew a large photograph album. 'Look,' she said putting it down on the far end of the table so that they all had to get up to look at it. She turned over the pages rapidly and then stood back. 'Look,' she said again.

A postcard-sized photograph took up one page. It showed a man and a girl on the deck of a yacht, smiling, quite contented with each other. A proud, peaceful, almost complacent air made it plain that they were father and daughter, and on a lifebelt was the large, white word 'Ermyn'.

'That's my mother,' said Michael, 'and my grandfather.'

'Was it his yacht?' asked Edward.

'How fascinating,' said Angela. 'Look, Ermyn.'

'I don't think I knew that,' said Henry. 'Did any of you know?'

'It could have been worse,' said Rose. 'It could have been the *Saucy Nancy* or the *Skylark*. It's funny,' she said, 'to call a baby after a boat.'

Ermyn looked at her own name, curved against the vastness of the sea. It was dangerous to write things down, to put a sign where nothing had been before. Her mother should never have left her – should never have just named her and then abandoned her to the nannies and the au pairs who had peopled her childhood, bored and neglectful, or curious and meddlesome; the big-legged ladies with their eye on Father; the occasional teacher probing her motherlessness with professional interest. Somewhere in a great space a baby doll was crying mechanically again and again 'Mama, Mama', forlorn and unanswerable. 'The ermine is merely the stoat in winter,' she said dolefully.

'I'm surprised your father didn't call you Alice after his mother,' said Angela. Rose was surprised too. The dying woman must have made her wishes clear in a crowded room – told the doctor, the vicar, the weeping servants.

How angry the Captain would have been, baulked at the last by his sad and fanciful wife departing beyond the reach of retribution.

Rose remembered the Captain's wife – tall, stately and unhappy in woollen stockings and pleated skirts. All the village knew about her – knew the Captain didn't love her, went off with fancy women, had only married her for her money. She never did learn how to manage him. Ermyn had been her final mistake, fatal as it turned out. Even Rose's mother, who on the whole disapproved of the upper classes as being flighty and immoral – shiftless, feckless and idle – had felt a certain sympathy for the Captain's wife. There was something pathetic about the large quiet woman, who wanted only to be good, harassed and driven by her husband's scorn, like a gentle lumbering pet set free in the wild.

'It's charming,' said Angela. 'You should frame it, Ermyn.'

Ermyn turned over the pages slowly. She paused at a picture of the Captain and his friends up on the moors with their guns. They lounged, laughing, in the heather, casually, conceitedly immortal. The Captain held a metal mug and stared, smiling, at the camera, daring it to catch him. And where was he now? Not quite alive in the photograph and not quite dead in bed. There were his enormous friends, Tiny and Sandy and Boy. How unprepared they looked. Perhaps death was progressive and all those people were now not merely older, but deader, than they had been.

'What a fat baby,' said Rose. 'Good heavens, it's you, Michael.'

There were no pictures of Ermyn.

Phyllis beckoned to Rose. She drew her into the hall and whispered something to her.

Rose grimaced. 'You'd better ring the doctor,' she said.

'What is it?' asked Angela. 'What's happened?'

'Nothing,' said Rose. 'Phyllis will telephone.'

'But why?' asked Angela. 'Rose, do tell me what's happening.'

'Nothing,' said Rose again.

'I'll go up,' said Angela.

'No need,' said Phyllis, barring the way.

Impotently, Angela retreated. She couldn't understand how it had come about that she should be prevented from showing herself at her best – kindly, practical, efficient. She went back to Edward, who was aware of her superiority.

Rose saw them sitting close together as she passed the drawing-room. Angela had been different recently, like a woman who had read that sex was good for her – not merely enjoyable but beneficial, like cod-liver oil: it would make her happier and more beautiful, and she was determined to have some.

Rose stopped. 'Has Michael taken up squash?' she asked on impulse.

'Yes,' said Angela, staring. 'He's rather keen on it. Why?'

'Oh nothing,' said Rose, who had noticed that as middle age approached many men regretted that they had never been sufficiently good at games and many women that they hadn't had sufficient lovers.

She remarked on this to Henry, who was coming out of the study.

'There's something like that in Hesiod,' he said reflectively, 'about mid-summer – the time when women are over-sexed and men are feeble. Perhaps he was thinking of middle age too.'

'I expect so,' said Rose, storing away the information for future use like a beachcomber.

Those old Welsh poets seemed to have covered everything, thought Ermyn, wandering past and wondering what to do.

The doctor came and went again quite soon. He smiled and waved at Angela, so there was obviously no immediate crisis. 'Ah, Annabel,' he said. 'Looking forward to the match?'

Rose went to lay the dining-room table for dinner: ritual preparation for an event not unassociated with death. The mahogany shone fox-red: the glasses were crystal clear as mountain streams and the plates as ferociously white as carnivorous teeth. The wild flowers of the saint's lamb stood in the middle of the table in a Ching vase. When Angela saw them she said to herself, 'Really, Rose has no idea', and she went to the garden and picked some roses and some dahlias to enliven the effect. Rose took them away again later and not a word was said.

*　　*　　*

Ermyn wandered erratically round the stable yard, unsettled and unsatisfied. She poked at the ivy, and a scatter of dead leaves and flies dropped out. She curved her hand gently round a head of hydrangea and folded a leaf again and again until the sap ran. She scuffed a piece of gravel under her shoe along the slate flags, making a horrid

111

sound. There was another sound – the buzzing of a bumble-bee caught in a web in the ivy. She thought it was screaming for help as it thrashed about. Already the spider was scuttling towards it, eager to collect the belated delivery. Rose would say, let matters take their course – she was always telling Jack to lay off the insecticide and stop interfering with the balance of nature. But Ermyn couldn't stand by. She broke the web with a twig, and the spider sped back to the shadows, while the bee dropped to the ground, still bound in sticky threads. Ermyn helped it as much as she could with two twigs, but the bee buzzed ever more hysterically. So she left it to calm itself.

It was hot and Ermyn was sweating. The stable door was open, and inside it was dark and dusty with old hay. She stood on the threshold, caught in a moment's startling exhilaration, which ebbed slowly as her eyes became accustomed to the dark.

'Hi,' said a blurred voice from a far corner.

'Oh, it's you,' said Ermyn. 'You should be working. Your grandmother thinks you are.'

'Silly old cow,' said the voice. 'Too hot.' He stretched out and reached up his hands to a dust-laden fall of sunlight. 'Waiting for Michael,' he said. 'He said he'd help me.'

'Don't lie,' said Ermyn, and then was ashamed. Phyllis always called them by their first names, but Gomer had never before called them anything. She was afraid of seeming snobbish.

'He did,' said Gomer.

'That was nice of *Michael*,' said Ermyn carefully.

'Wasn't it,' said Gomer, 'wasn't it *nice* of Michael.'

'You're drunk,' said Ermyn, as the particular quality of the voice's imprecision became clear.

'Sod off.' He rolled unexpectedly off a bench and on to the straw-strewn floor.

'Don't talk to me like that,' said Ermyn. 'I'll tell your grandmother.'

'Oh don't,' pleaded Gomer mockingly. 'She'll give me a row.'

He shuffled on to his hands and knees and gazed at her, his small, shiny eyes fixed in the stare of the drunk – concentrated, searching.

'I'll show you something,' he said, crooking his finger. 'C'm 'ere.'

Ermyn went towards him suspiciously, expecting perhaps a dead bat, or a frog.

'What?' she asked.

'Look.' He pushed aside several empty beer cans and reached under the bench. He brought out a magazine, and it fell open. 'Look,' he said again.

The window high in the wall above them, out of the reach of flailing hooves, let in a dim but sufficient light. Ermyn stared at the page before her. For a long moment it meant nothing. The word 'Rose' was deeply scored in pencil on one large buttock.

Above, on the slates, she could hear the comic incongruous sound of birds walking. She looked up slowly. Gomer was watching her and grinning.

She dropped the magazine and went out. Her sense of identity with the human race, never very strong, suffered a further lesion. Better be one of the sheep cropping beyond the fence at the unprotesting turf, better be one of the sullen rocks holding back the mountain, better even

113

be the bluebottle musing over a sheep turd under the hydrangea – better be anything than part of that multiple monster. Perhaps she belonged with the backward people, smiling and starting in the lane.

'Gomer's ill,' she said to Rose in the kitchen. 'He's drunk in the stable.'

'Hush,' said Rose. 'Phyllis is in the scullery.' She spoke sharply. When Phyllis was upset the washing-machine mysteriously choked, the dish-washer bit the dishes in half, the refrigerator flung open its door, baring its contents to ruinous warmth. 'Don't fuss,' she said, but she looked angrily at the kitchen door. Alcohol was a useful weapon. She had learnt a lot by sitting soberly and listening, hospitably pressing the port on dizzied guests, suddenly convinced that they had waited all their lives to confide in someone as understanding as Rose. Out of her control, it was nothing but a nuisance, and Gomer was supposed to be clearing the pavilion. She wondered where he was getting the money from; his grandmother kept him rather short in his own best interests.

'What *is* wrong?' asked Angela, coming to find a clean ashtray for Edward.

'Nothing,' said Rose, without a thought for Ermyn's troubled face.

'Did those photographs upset you?' asked Angela kindly. 'You must just remember your mother and grandfather were happy then.'

Ermyn went white.

'Gracious,' said Angela. 'I wouldn't have thought it would upset you like that. You poor *child*.'

Ermyn shuddered convulsively, neck to waist.

'Sit down,' said Angela. 'I'll make you some tea.'

114

Phyllis came up the scullery steps, carrying a tray full of depressing sick-room utensils with spouts, and glanced at Ermyn without interest. She looked unusually cheerful and walked briskly, her short efficient movements speeded up by pleasant anticipation.

'All ready for the match then?' she said. Gomer considered himself extremely good. He had told his *nain* so, and she believed him, her native incredulity powerless against the force of her affection.

'There,' said Angela putting a cup before Ermyn. 'There are two sugars in it. Drink it up while it's hot.'

Ermyn didn't take sugar, but she sipped the nauseous solution bravely, incapable of rebuffing a kindness.

Angela sat down by her and patted her hand. '*Poor child*,' she said agreeably in the tone she used to her mother's dogs.

When Ermyn had drunk her tea Angela went back to Edward in the drawing-room. 'Edward,' she called.

She turned round twice and even looked behind the sofa, but he had gone. Frowning, she went into the garden and sat on the grass. It was Rose's fault. If Rose were only better organised and would remember each even ing to put out the drinks at the same time, he wouldn't have to go off to the pub. She didn't often have the chance to talk to someone as interesting and intelligent as Edward.

When Edward came back everyone had gathered on the terrace. He was angry. Even out of earshot as he walked up the path he was fulminating against the Irish, one of whom had that day been apprehended on the train from Holyhead with a small suitcase full of explosives.

'Savages,' he grumbled, spitting a little, his brows

115

drawn together behind his spectacles. 'Killing our finest young men. Coming over here murdering innocent women and children. Ignorant savages.'

'I am Irish myself,' said Rose, embarrassing everyone with her tactlessness.

Angela pursed her lips. Rose didn't look Irish, she didn't sound Irish, she hadn't ever been to that wretched island. She was contrary.

'The Irish don't *like* the English,' explained Rose.

'That doesn't mean they can go round murdering innocent people,' said someone.

'I can't, at the moment, think of a better reason,' said Rose.

'Salt of the earth,' said Edward, speaking of the English.

Perhaps the salt of the earth has lost its savour, thought Ermyn, who had given up trying to read the Bible from start to finish and instead just read whatever page it fell open at. Wherewith shall the salt be salted? She could almost taste the insipid salt, diluted tears, arid sweat and blood.

'None of you are English,' said Rose kindly. 'You're all Welsh, except for Edward, and he's Scotch.'

'Scots,' said Michael, prissily.

'Scottish,' said Edward.

'Oh, I forgot you, Angela,' said Rose. 'I'm frightfully sorry.'

'Don't bother about me,' said Angela angrily. '*I* can look after *myself*.' The Captain's family would sooner have admitted to a strain of hobgoblin, or even jew, than the kind of Welsh Rose was implying, and there was no dignified way of saying so. Henry was impossible. He didn't seem to mind whatever Rose said. He was looking at her now with a perfectly idiotic smile. 'Henry looks terribly English,' Angela said.

'He doesn't,' said Rose, feigning indignation. 'The typically English face is set in the Churchillian or potato mould – a large pale mass with small features starting high up in the brow and arranged in a vertical line, stopping well short of the chin, which then either slopes into the collar or bulges forward according to some genetic chance with which I am not familiar. Except for recent Conservative prime ministers, of course. They mostly look like bunnies.'

'What *do* you do for an encore?' asked Angela getting up in a flounce. 'I can smell something burning. Are we ever going to eat? I'm starving, and you all just sit here talking nonsense.'

*   *   *

Rose gave Edward an extra egg. 'To keep up his strength,' she explained.

'We mustn't eat too much,' said Henry. 'We must be fresh for tomorrow.'

'It isn't much,' said Rose. 'Just this, and some duck and a little bit of pudding.'

'Duck?' said Edward, water streaming around his teeth. He put half an egg into his mouth.

'Duck, my darling?' said Henry. 'That seems rather a bad omen for a cricket match.'

'Edward's very good at cricket,' Rose told Ermyn. 'He was in the First XI at school. Isn't that so, Michael?'

Michael, whose failure to attain this status still sometimes haunted his dreams, as Rose was well aware, winced a little. He would have been glad, at this moment, to have heard his father's opinion of Edward. Weedy little chap. Egg-head.

'I saw a collared dove yesterday,' he said. 'They're getting more common.'

'Are they?' said Ermyn.

'Common?' asked Rose. 'Coo, pardon?'

'I've always been fond of bird-watching,' Michael went on. 'Since I was quite small. I don't know why.'

'Fraud has it . . .' began Rose.

'Freud,' Angela corrected.

'She calls psycho-analysis Freudulent conversion,' said Henry fondly.

'Very funny,' said Angela. 'Ha ha.'

'Fraud says,' continued Rose, 'that it springs from the desire to witness the primal scene.'

'*What* primal scene?' asked Angela, laughing crossly.

'The copulation of one's parents,' explained Rose, her eyes lowered. 'I don't believe they taught you anything at Roedean.'

'I wasn't *at* Roedean,' said Angela.

Michael was offended at this unhealthy interpretation of his hobby. 'I don't believe that,' he said. 'I've always had a passion for bird-watching, and egg-collecting. Father knew the countryside inside out. He always told us never to take more than one egg.'

He should have told Edward, thought Ermyn, watching him. She laughed and choked uncomfortably on a crumb.

'He *did*,' said Michael, irritably. 'You're too young to remember.'

'I didn't mean . . .' said Ermyn.

'The English don't have passions,' said Rose. 'They

118

have *tastes*: for porcelain and flagellation, and Georgian porticos – things like that. But of course,' she said, smiting her brow gently, 'you're not English. I keep forgetting.'

'She says Freud's problems were purely psycho-semitic,' said Henry, laughing alone.

There was no sunset. The sun merely departed, like a neglected guest drawing on an old mackintosh. The garden lay characterless and glum, rinsed grey by evening.

' I think I'll light the candles,' said Rose.

'It may brighten up in the morning,' said Henry. He poured out the wine, filling the glasses rather more than was usual, and got up to carve the ducks.

'Give Edward plenty of skin,' said Rose. She added another lump of butter to the potatoes, and pushed them towards him.

'Drink up,' she said. 'It's really quite cold.'

'Tell me about your children,' said Angela, leaning sideways and looking into Edward's face. 'Are you sending them to your school?'

'Yes,' said Edward, who doubted whether he'd be able to afford it.

'Are you sure it's wise?' asked Rose.

'What?' said Edward, his mind running painfully in circles. All those thousands and thousands of pounds.

'It will be expensive,' said Angela, 'but worth it.'

'It's a pity about the grammar schools,' said Henry. 'Rose was very well taught, but the twins will have to go to St Hilary's.'

'Annoying,' said Angela shortly, feeling again a familiar bitterness at the treachery of a system that had given Rose, free, an education as good as her own – which had cost, over the years, as much as a small house. 'Those days

119

have gone,' she said, rallying. 'The quality of state education is quite dreadful. Lexie is still at a state primary, and that isn't too bad at the moment, but he'll have to go to prep school next year when he's nine, or he'll never learn a thing.'

'Consider the sexual implications,' said Rose.

'Oh, what now?' said Michael languidly, pushing aside his plate. 'You're always talking about sex.'

'Not always,' said Rose. She assumed an intense, Viennese expression. 'Think,' she said. 'Locking children of one sex up together is bad enough in the latency period and can lead to all sorts of psychic malfunctioning, but after puberty it is deplorably unwholesome, and homosexuality is the almost invariable result. Part of the trouble stems from the blurring of the confines of pedagogy and pederasty. No one but a lunatic or a moral degenerate would choose to spend his working life with a load of children, so the attitude – unreal, unnatural and more than a little barmy – is inevitably perpetuated.'

'What nonsense,' cried Michael, infuriated.

'Homosexuals are no different from the rest of us,' said Angela.

'Oh they are, they are,' said Rose. 'Quite, quite different.'

'We are all fifty per cent gay,' said Angela sternly.

'I have noticed,' said Rose, 'that people in this country always assume that everyone has something to hide. I think it reflects rather badly on them. Whenever some eminent figure is discovered in a scandalous situation, sooner or later an Anglican clergyman is sure to remark that there are areas in all our lives that we wouldn't care to have too closely scrutinised. But then, as they seem to

120

spend so much of their time in public lavatories, one can see they might feel like that.

'That just shows they're normal,' said Angela.

'Putting one's organ through a hole in a lavatory partition wouldn't be precisely my definition of normal,' said Rose.

'Is that what they do?' asked Henry, interested.

'Seriously, Rose,' said Angela, pale with temper. 'If you had a son and he turned out to be homosexual, what would *you* do?'

'Shoot him,' said Rose after a moment's consideration.

There was immediate protest at this illiberal remark.

'I do wish you'd stop trying to be clever, Rose.'

'What on earth do you know about morality, Rose?'

'Only what I read,' said Rose. 'When a baronet is discovered behind a bush in the park with a guardsman, or a minister of the crown is caught creeping out of the country with his socks stuffed full of bank notes and a woman not his wife ten paces behind, or a public person is revealed disporting himself with a couple of tarts and a teddy bear in West Paddington, they complain to the press that the outcry is hypocritical and that everyone would like to do what they were doing if only they had the wit and imagination, the money or the chance. They regard the law as the instrument of envy, like nationalisation and death duties.'

'They're right. People are only human,' said Angela.

'Speak for yourself,' said Rose.

'You're hopelessly out of date, Rose. All those old ideas of morality are hopelessly out of date. Besides what about *Labour*? I suppose you're one of those people who think everyone on the Left is perfect.' She stared at Rose in-

121

quisitorially, like a rather stupid magistrate.

'Certainly not,' said Rose. 'I think they're mostly mad.'

'There you go again,' said Angela.

'They'd all jump at a coronet at the drop of a cloth cap,' said Rose; 'swap their Brothers for their Peers without a backward glance. The historical sequence is quite simple, really,' she continued, warming to her theme. 'The first catastrophe was the Reformation. The Reformation led to the Industrial Revolution. The Industrial Revolution created the British Empire. The British Empire necessitated the Public Schools. The Public Schools engendered the Class System. The Class System made Socialism inevitable. And Socialism – which by bad luck arrived just as it couldn't be afforded – brought about the collapse of the economy.'

'I shall vote Liberal next time,' said Angela virtuously.

'A Liberal is just a Conservative who's been left out in the rain,' Rose told her.

'You have no respect for anyone, Rose,' said Angela. 'You should think of Lord Thing sometimes, a really *good* man. Someone who has *everything* and still thinks of the less fortunate.'

Rose thought of Lord Thing. He devoted much of his time to holding the bloodstained hands of the nastier, madder murderers, quite properly incarcerated in high-security gaols more or less safe from the vengeance of a profoundly offended populace. He longed to get them out for reasons obscure to everyone but himself.

'Lord Thing is a *voyee*,' said Rose. 'He is drawn irresistibly to where the light is strongest, even the light of disapprobation. People think he's a *voyeur*, but he isn't. He's worse. He doesn't feel himself to be present unless all

122

eyes are upon *him*. He sees himself in a priestly or godly role, able to forgive sins, forgetting that the only sins people are able to forgive are those committed against themselves.'

'What rubbish, Rose,' said Angela. 'He's a truly humble man. You should read his book on Self-abnegation.'

'This current cynicism about our leadership is most unhealthy,' said Edward. 'There are some extremely able men at the top. You must remember, politics is a very taxing business . . .' He had made this joke in his column a few weeks before and it had gone down well. Now he waited until Angela had laughed and congratulated him and then continued. 'The hours our politicians have to keep in the House inevitably have a bad effect on their home lives. Research has shown that most top politicians keep mistresses or have recourse to prostitutes – both here and in America.' He spoke regretfully, but without censure.

'Well, I think adultery is a filthy habit,' said Rose, 'like using someone else's toothbrush.'

Angela looked up, directly at Rose, and went a dark wine-red. 'What a horrible idea,' she said, her voice failing with anger.

Ermyn thought Angela would get up and run out of the room, she looked so disturbed. No one else had heard Rose's last remark. Edward was pursuing a pool of gravy over his plate, and Henry and Michael were talking of some past event to do with money.

'If you think so little of the English,' said Angela to Rose, 'I can't think why you stay here.'

'This is Wales,' said Rose reasonably.

'Oh, what a silly conversation,' said Angela, recovering, and turning her chair to talk to Henry and Michael.

123

They glanced up briefly as she spoke, and then went on talking to each other, earnestly and not in total agreement.

'Who are you talking about?' asked Rose.

'Cousin Teddy,' said Michael shortly.

Henry lit a cigar. 'He's just contributed an essay to a book questioning the divinity of Christ.'

'They do that,' said Rose.

'You can't blame him,' said Henry. 'He's in a dilemma. While he realises that if he doesn't believe in Christ he can't stay in the Church, he feels that if he does he can hardly be in a university.'

'Tough,' said Rose. Teddy had had his doubts even before he fell on his head. She took away the plates and passed round bowls of chocolate mousse smothered in heavy cream. A rich cheese and the decanter of port waited menacingly on the sideboard.

Ermyn began to feel dizzy. She had drunk and eaten everything she was offered, and the mention of Teddy brought another image before her eyes. She could see him beating slowly with a monstrous steel teaspoon at his own white fragile skull.

After a few spoonfuls of mousse they began to talk again. The words marched around in Ermyn's head, taking on a life and meaning of their own. As they made sense they formed into regiments and battalions – blind murderous little creatures coming together to destroy and mutilate – and everything her family spoke of fell apart as she listened. In all the smoky warmth and light, the plenitude of food and drink, there was no good will. Somewhere someone who loved her better would take her away: take her somewhere so high the broad shifting back of the wind would brush against the soles of her feet; offer her the icy water riven into strands, uniting again to stream against her outstretched arms, the cold bone of her head; offer her the huge cold empty air . . . It must have been from an evening like this that the saint had fled. If she were here she would be disgusted, would embark on one of the tirades for which she was famous. It was said she could utter commination for an hour without once repeating herself. Perhaps even now she was turning irritably in her grave, drawing the cold stone cover close to her contemptuous mouth . . .

Ermyn began to say she thought she'd go to bed but said, 'I'm going to die.'

No one heard her except Angela, who merely remarked, 'Don't be silly, darling.' Nevertheless Ermyn felt as though she had suddenly become enormously large and was illuminated from all sides. She crouched and glared at the candle glow.

Next to Rose Edward had fallen asleep, his head on the table, a few wisps of mousy hair mingling with some cheese rinds.

'Edward has a theory that public school boys are better-looking than others, and the better the school, the better-looking the boy,' said Rose. 'Has he told you about it?'

Edward opened his eyes at the mention of his name. 'To seek to excel in all things and to be superior to others. The Homeric ideal. That's the point of the public school system.'

'You spoke well of the Sermon on the Mount last time you were here,' said Rose lowering her own head to the table to look at him. 'I would so like to know how you reconcile those two points of view?'

Ermyn forced herself to sit upright. 'If you'll excuse me,' she said indistinctly, 'I'll go to bed. Goodnight.'

'Goodnight,' they said.

'If Ermyn would diet and do something about her hair she'd be quite attractive,' remarked Angela, as the door closed.

'Port?' invited Henry. The dining-room clock chimed. It had a foolish, effeminate voice and they ignored it. The Captain always liked the ladies to leave the table at this stage, and in her own house Angela would have led the ladies upstairs to the bathroom; but Rose sat on and Angela stayed too.

'Father always said a woman's most important points were her neck, legs and thumbs,' said Michael.

'*Thumbs?*' said Angela. 'I never heard that before.'

'It sounds like the fowl on boxing day,' said Henry.

'He was only speaking of ladies,' said Rose. 'He liked his *women* to have big fat bottoms.'

Edward sat up. 'That was delicious,' he said, with apolaustic relish. 'Could I have a little more of that awfully good cheese, please.'

*   *   *

Ermyn climbed carefully upstairs, placing her feet with great deliberation on the slippery treads. Rose was full of Superbia. It was pride that made her so relentless. 'Superbia, Superbia,' said Ermyn to herself at each step. 'Oh *Rose.*'

Greed? That was Edward. Lechery? Ermyn blushed, even alone in the darkness; she knew without thinking who that was – Angela, moist-lipped at Edward. Avarice?

126

All the village – and Michael: he was a very good businessman. Envy was Phyllis, consumed with bitter, doomed hopes for her grandson – and he was Sloth. There was a seventh sin, thought Ermyn. Anger lay in the room ahead of her, burnt out by its own furious force. Poor Father. She stopped by his door, wished him well, and then went into her bedroom.

The room was unchanged since her childhood. A striped Welsh tweed rug covered her bed, and on it sat an oddly immaculate teddy bear next to a doll which had been bought for her six months too late when her painful longing for it had passed. On her dressing-table were an unused manicure set given to her by an aunt years ago to encourage her to stop biting her nails, a row of glass animals and another framed photograph of Rose and Henry getting into a car on their wedding day. They were both smiling, and Henry looked well pleased with his prize, but Ermyn was overcome by a strange feeling that nothing would have persuaded her to get into that car with Rose. Her mind filled with the idea of a wild and terrible thrashing: a sudden, absolute, crimson-soaked silence, and Rose still smiling, dark stains on her lovely mouth, the creamy lace steaming with fresh blood. Hate? enquired Ermyn of the silence. She hates us?

Ermyn shook her head despairingly, and closed her eyes. At that the world went round and she opened them again hurriedly. Outside the window she could see the leaves of the sycamore dancing desultorily in the breeze against the night sky – like tired children driven on by an unkind but preoccupied master, and time and again, not in her imagination, but clearly before her eyes, she saw Gomer's magazine. She had led, as do many unloved children, a sheltered existence, and now she felt that she had let into her mind something evil and unclean like a rat, which would never go away but only grow larger and worse. She thought she must be very bad to feel like this. Badness washed around her like dirty water.

She crossed the landing to look at the sea. It was black and bitter and it was moaning to itself. She tried some of the books that still stood on her shelves, but she had never been permitted the flavourless fiction that children enjoy, and Grimm, Hans Andersen and Lewis Carroll were no sort of specific against dismay. Eventually she picked up her bible again. It fell open at Judges 19, and she read it. She grew quite calm as she read – calm and very cold. The story began somewhat oddly, but then the Bible always seemed a bit odd.

A Levite and his concubine were going off on a trip, perhaps a little holiday. That was nice. They stayed with the damsel's father for a while and their hearts were merry. Then they went on until the sun went down upon them when they were by Gibeah which belongeth to Benjamin. All right, except that they couldn't find any-where to stay. But then a dear old gentleman said he would put them up. 'Only lodge not in the street,' he said kindly. They fed the asses, and washed their own feet, and their hearts were merry again. Then the music changed. There came certain sons of Belial who beset the house round about and beat at the door saying, 'Bring forth the man that came into thine house that we may know him.' Even Ermyn could tell that this was not as friendly as it sounded, and the old man obviously knew what they were after. He said, 'Behold, here is my daughter, a maiden, and his concubine; them I will bring out now, and humble ye them, and do with them what seemeth good unto you: but unto this man do not so vile a thing.' Well, really, thought Ermyn, that *is* carrying hospitality a bit far. Then they took the concubine and knew her and abused her all the night until the morning; and when the day began to spring they let her go. She went back in the dawning of the day and fell down at the door of the man's house where her lord was, till it was light and her lord rose up in the morning and opened the doors of the house – perhaps to fetch in the milk and the morning papers – and behold, the woman his concubine was fallen down at the door of the house, and her hands were upon the threshold. He said to her, 'Up and let us be going', but none answered. So then the man took her home on an ass and divided her, together with her bones, into twelve pieces, and sent her into all the coasts of Israel. He was obviously annoyed and the children of Israel were very shocked, as well they might be.

But Ermyn read no more. She closed the book carefully, and turned out her light. She knew where she was now; there was no comfort and no love, not anywhere.

After a while she fell asleep, to a distant rumble of thunder, which sounded as though the bald-topped mountains had broken loose and were rolling slowly together.

* * *

Downstairs Rose was becoming bored. She hardly ever drank, and the others had all grown bemused, passing beyond her influence into that state of weary intoxication where long-held personal grievances burgeon, hidden pre-

129

occupations swell to exclude all sense of other people and dialogue ceases entirely.

'. . . and he said I had the loveliest body he'd ever known,' Angela was saying openly, to Edward – who was simultaneously telling her that if the middle class didn't make a stand for decency and culture and family life the country was finished.

'Keep it up, keep it up at all costs,' said Michael. 'The cricket match is one of the highspots of the year.'

'Ooh,' cried Angela, falling slightly sideways and gripping Edward's arm, her expression of winsome lewdness hidden by her ladylike hair.

'We owe it to the village,' said Michael.

'*Noblesse oblige*,' whispered Rose.

'I'm fed up with it,' said Henry frankly, 'and it makes a lot of extra work for Rose.'

'I don't mind,' said Rose truthfully.

'Schport, schportsmanschip,' said Edward just before falling asleep again.

Rose took the few remaining glasses out to the scullery. 'Oh, finished, have you?' said Phyllis unpleasantly.

'Yes, thank you,' said Rose. There was no need at all for Phyllis to stay up. No one ever asked her to. She sat by the range, her stockings rolled down to her knees and a man's sweater clutched over her chest.

'I hope Gomer had an early night,' said Rose. 'I know Henry's relying on him very strongly tomorrow.'

Her tone was earnest and warm, and Phyllis relaxed. She knew Rose's insincerity, but was satisfied to see the formalities observed. 'He'll be all right,' she said, getting up.

'Oh *good*,' said Rose.

* * *

Rose went rather sleepily up the stairs, pleased with herself. It seemed unlikely that anyone from the *Plâs* would play very successfully tomorow. She had planned a supper for them, unctuous with consolation and with strong invalid overtones.

Suddenly, on the landing, she stopped. The light was on in the twins' room, and the door stood open. Perhaps Death had come for them – had felt in their beds and, finding nothing, turned on the light, the better to look for them. She bounded forward to confront him.

Angela stood in the middle of the room gazing round, her arms full of sheets.

'Jesus, Mary and Joseph,' said Rose.

'I thought you'd gone to bed,' said Angela. 'I think Edward should sleep in here tonight. You've put him so far away from us and he isn't well at all.'

Rose stared at her open-mouthed, imagining Edward's breath in the morning. The twins' breath smelt of air barely touched with apples and milk, their flesh compounded of something between meat and peach.

'I got these from the linen room,' said Angela, indicating the sheets, 'but I see the beds have been made up.' She sounded surprised, being unable to rid herself of the notion that Rose was one of those unfeminine sluts who bring womanhood into disrepute and that one day she would catch her out – washing socks in the sugar bowl perhaps, or putting coal in the bread bin.

'No,' said Rose, when she felt able to speak. 'You mustn't disorient him. He knows his way from that room like a hen on a chalk line. If you move him about, he'll

131

fall downstairs, or get into bed with Phyllis.' She seized the sheets from Angela fiercely so that there was no time for argument. They were the linen, monogrammed ones that Rose kept for her own room.

'I think you're very mean,' said Angela childishly, foiled and petulant.

Rose stood by the door until she'd gone out and followed her along the passage. The door of the green bedroom was open and it was adequately lit by the bed-side lamps, which were held by two simpering, sinuous china ladies, but Michael wasn't in it.

"Night,' said Angela abruptly, and closed the door.

Henry was reading the paper in bed.

'Where's Michael?' asked Rose.

'Michael?' said Henry, still reading.

'Your brother,' said Rose. 'Your brother, Michael.'

'I don't know,' said Henry. 'I expect he's gone to bed.'

Rose opened the window, and shivered – more with faint shock than the cold. She missed the twins. Before they were born, she had never known anxiety or even fear. The world had held no terrors for her, but a world in which the twins could co-exist with the possibility of harm was not the place she had previously supposed it to be, and sometimes she grew angry with both, the world and the twins, that they should conspire to alarm her so.

'If Michael's still out,' she said – deceitfully, for this was not what she was thinking – 'I hope he remembers to lock up.'

*　　*　　*

132

The morning of the cricket match dawned dust-grey and saddening. The sky had an unkempt, disordered look and was littered untidily with a few tattered, discoloured clouds. A shabby wind blew sporadically from every quarter, and the sea had the rough pinched appearance of the pebble-dashed council houses that so detracted from the beauty of Llanelys. It was featureless, confusing weather.

'Nice morning,' said Phyllis, determined to see a bright side to the day on which Gomer would shine. And indeed to her besotted, and none too particular, eyes the day looked as good as any other.

Bacon cracked brazenly in the frying pan, and three of the finest tomatoes waited with two large brown eggs at the side of the stove: sacrifices to Gomer's appetite. Phyllis made no attempt to hide them, and no apology. She felt none was due – Gomer deserved the best, and its provenance was immaterial.

'Give him some fried bread,' said Rose.

'How nice,' said Angela, 'I'll do my own egg, Phyllis. I know how I like it.'

When it was cooked she chose the largest rasher of bacon and sat down at the head of the table to eat it. Alcohol always made her hungry.

Ermyn came down next, looking tired and plain and indefinably dirty, as though she'd been badly washed. She sat down and absentmindedly sipped Phyllis's tea.

'It's got sugar in it,' she said, surprised. 'Oh, I'm sorry Phyllis. Is it yours?' She put it down, but made no effort to get a cup for herself.

'Here comes Gomer for his breakfast,' said Rose. 'Move along, Ermyn.'

Ermyn got up very quickly, knocking over her chair.

133

'I'm going for a walk,' she said.

She stepped away as Gomer came in. There was at least a table's width between them, but it wasn't enough for Ermyn, who backed away like a sheep before a dog.

Phyllis watched this performance with eyes grown hard and motionless. 'Got very posh all of a sudden,' she said. But Gomer grimaced and touched his finger to his forehead out of Rose's sight, and his grandmother grimaced back, reassured.

'Brrr,' said Angela rubbing her bare arms under the yellow cashmere cardigan slung over her shoulders. '*Not* garden-party weather.'

'Go on,' said Phyllis. 'Lovely day.'

'Her blood's got thin,' explained Rose. 'It's all that time she spends on the Costa Brava.'

'I have never been to the Costa Brava in my life,' said Angela distinctly. Rose knew perfectly well that when they went to Spain they stayed with diplomatic friends of her father's outside Seville.

'I been there,' said Gomer, politely ejecting a bit of tomato skin on to his plate.

'I'm sure you have,' said Angela, gazing out of the window and wondering why Rose let him eat in the kitchen.

'Going again too,' said Gomer.

'Lucky old you,' said Angela, as tiredly cutting as if he'd been one of themselves, graciousness extinguished by her hangover.

Phyllis filled a tray for the dish-washer with slow deliberation. On to it went a crazed but beautiful blue-and-white cup that was never used. 'Dirty old thing,' she said.

134

Rose watched it go with regret. It would not come out entire.

'Coffee,' said Michael, tottering in theatrically, clutching his brow. 'Hot, black coffee. Oh God,' he added humorously dropping into a chair and thrusting out his feet. Apart from cloth mules he wore only a short matching dressing-gown.

'Couldn't you have dressed?' asked Angela quietly, looking at her newspaper.

Ermyn came in and sat down next to Rose. Gomer stared at her until she looked back. Then he began to wink and leer and indicate something to his left by contorting his mouth and eyebrows. Unwittingly she followed his glance. She could only see Michael lying back in a rocking-chair in a short dressing-gown. What a stupid boy Gomer was . . . A very short dressing-gown . . .

Michael got up and crossed to the table, put his hand on Gomer's shoulder and leaned across to reach for the sugar. Under Michael's stomach Gomer grinned at Ermyn – a bright, wide, triumphant grin. Ermyn stared back uncomprehendingly, Angela rustled her newspaper irritably as the sugar bowl brushed it. Rose swept some crumbs from the table as Henry and Edward came in. There was nothing here to grin about with such lunatic ardour. She looked away again. Michael sat down. Gomer finished his breakfast. Only Phyllis stood, unnaturally still, in the scullery doorway.

'Well, I can't sit here all day,' said Rose in workman-like tones. 'I'm going down to look at the hut and see how tidy Gomer has made it.' She smiled at him falsely.

'I was at it till after midnight,' said Gomer smugly.

'Thought you went to bed early?' said his *nain.*

135

'Got up again, didn't I?' said Gomer. 'Just to finish off properly.'

*　　　*　　　*

The Elysian Field lay just beyond the garden, level with the lower lawn but separated from it by a hedge of hazel and alder and hawthorn and a small threadlike stream. It was a dank and charmless meadow eternally troubled by a freakish wind that brought piles of litter to settle in the corners and drift aimlessly about. Father blamed the villagers for its constant untidiness, but Ermyn thought this was due to Elys Water ebbing and flowing, taking the tide with it. Rank weeds proliferated about its margins – nettles and plantain and goosegrass – and tall thistles sprang up just where the fielders would fall in them. It was haunted by the less attractive insects: hornets, sandflies, wasps and crane flies – tiresome things that left their jointed legs sticking to your clothes and hair and flew off lamed but uncomplaining.

At the far end a flock of seagulls quarrelled raucously over something dead, and as Ermyn pushed through the hedge two crows rose and flapped slowly away, black and mournfully shiny as funeral hats, their wings raggedly fringed.

'Ugh,' said Rose behind her, pushing aside the hawthorn branches. She stepped over the small stream and looked around. 'They must be mad,' she said. 'It isn't a playground.'

Ermyn carefully pushed the branches together. Father had always refused to have a gate cut in the boundary hedge although it was nearly a mile round by the road.

136

Rose went over to the pavilion and bent to feel for the key under the raised platform. It was quite safe there. Few visitors knew of the field's existence and it had never appealed to the locals as a suitable site for the rituals of vandalism or courtship.

Ermyn looked over her shoulder. The blind blankness of the place made her feel that somewhere there must be an unseen watcher. It was completely surrounded by trees and bushes, except for the narrow opening of the lane from the main road.

Rose pushed open the door, which creaked against the damp and ground on the grit that lay beneath it. Inside, the hut was dim and the windows grimy. It smelt of dust and paraffin, dead mice and mould. A pile of grocer's provisions stood on a trestle table.

'The little sod didn't sweep the floor,' said Rose, staring at the dull, furred boards.

'I'll do it,' said Ermyn.

Rose moved around a partition which screened a small sink and draining-board and passed out a broom.

It was all quite as unpleasant as Ermyn remembered, and for some reason this raised, rather than lowered, her spirits.

Rose pushed open the unwilling windows and forced the tap over the sink to turn. After a moment a brownish liquid began to trickle out. 'Water?' she surmised. She dampened a cloth in it and wiped over the trestle. 'Don't eat or drink anything here.'

Ermyn swept the dust into a pile and out through the open door. 'Angela's coming,' she said.

Rose breathed warily through the thin acrid cloud the broom had raised undefined in the sunless gloom.

'Horrors,' said Angela. 'When on earth was this place opened last? I don't believe Gomer's touched it at all.'

'He's been in here,' said Rose. An empty whisky bottle, some cigarette ends and two smeared wine glasses stood on the floor.

'You ought to keep all the drink absolutely locked up,' said Angela. 'It's a fearful temptation to a boy like that.'

'I do,' said Rose absently. 'At least, all the whisky's kept in the drawing-room and he'd never dare go in there.' The Captain had been quite clear about that and there were some rules that would never be broken. She stared at the dirty little still-life, wondering. It seemed as though something she knew nothing of was going on, and that was unusual.

'Well, I'd swear those glasses came from the house,' said Angela. She regarded the foodstuffs critically. 'We could easily have made cakes and sausage rolls and things in time if you'd thought about it, Rose. These are beastly.'

'We did that one year,' said Rose, 'and they thought it was because we couldn't afford to buy anything. They were very scornful.'

'Oh, nonsense,' said Angela, as a matter of course. 'I'll butter the bread.'

'Margarine,' said Rose. 'They like a nice smooth finish. No lumps.'

Angela unwrapped the bread. Limp, damp, stillborn, it folded without breaking and soaked up the sweet, lumpy, vinegary mixture called 'sandwich spread' which, Rose said, looked as though it had been eaten once already.

'They *like* it,' said Rose. 'You'll see. And there are little jars of potted beef and shrimp. Ermyn, you can unpack the swiss rolls and put out the assorted biscuits. There should be some plates in that cupboard. Then you can decorate the sandwiches with a bit of cress – not much, they won't eat it. Then later we'll warm up the sausage rolls and put out the crisps. Phyllis can make the tea. She knows how to work the urn.' She indicated this piece of apparatus, which had a stubborn spinsterish air, with a dismissive wave of her hand. She put out cardboard plates and cups on another trestle and surveyed the effect. 'Would you say it looked a little bleak?' she asked.

'Why not use the china?' suggested Angela.

'They'd break it,' said Rose.

'Shall I get some flowers?' offered Ermyn.

'There's one of those things in the china pantry,' said Rose. 'A cross between a soup tureen and a crematorium urn. Very disconcerting. They used to have them in cinemas with gladiolas in.'

'It's alabaster,' said Angela frostily. 'If that's the one you mean. I brought it from home years ago to decorate the top table at one of Father's dinners.'

'It's very decorative,' said Rose. 'Ermyn, go and pick some common roses. Middle-aged dark red ones, and some blowsy white ones. Not the very creamy ones like old ladies' faces.'

'It's absurd to talk about flowers like that,' rebuked Angela. 'Unscientific.'

They worked all morning, spreading wrung-out wet cloths over the sandwiches and paper napkins over the biscuits. The brown trickle from the tap had given way to a steady gush of fairly clean water. The *Plâs* got its water from a well up the mountain, fed by an underground stream, but the pavilion, like the rest of Llanelys,

139

relied on an inadequate reservoir full of tadpoles and seagull feathers, which sometimes came through the taps.

Ermyn found Jack and sent him for an extra six pints of milk, which he had forgotten, and when he brought them Rose sent him back for six bottles of orange squash, which he had also forgotten.

'You should make a list, Jack,' said Angela. 'Save yourself all that running about.'

'I don't mind,' said Jack. 'If we can't help lovely ladies, what can we do?'

Angela turned her back on him. He would never have spoken like that when the Captain was around.

'If you've got nothing better to do than stand there making half-witted remarks you can take all these boxes and packets and incinerate them,' said Rose. 'Or would you rather just fling them round the field?'

'Now you know I never did that,' said Jack the Liar good humouredly.

He squashed all the rubbish into a large cardboard box and went off with it. Angela wondered if there was any tactful way she could explain to Rose how not to speak to servants. That was the trouble with people like Rose. They never quite learned how to behave.

'We'd better get lunch over,' said Rose.

*   *   *

In previous years the Captain and his friends would have their lunch in the dining-room: bread and cheese and beer. The rest of the home team ate on the terrace. Then the Captain and his friends would go and play, and when they'd won they'd come back to an invariable supper of

Dee salmon and hock and raspberries and wax merry on port until very late.

Rose had decided to do it differently. Jack and Gomer should join them and they'd eat in the kitchen, and as lunch was a more formal meal than breakfast they'd have it standing up to prevent any awkwardness. It would seem natural and democratic, and Angela would loathe it. The rest of the team could find their own lunch and arrive just in time for the game. The Captain's affliction would make this appear reasonable, and while there would be some ill-feeling it would not be overt.

Phyllis was energetically flicking a cloth at some crumbs and acknowledged them as they came in. 'Ready,' she said.

'Very nice,' said Rose. 'Very colourful.'

Pink ham, crimson beetroot, lettuce and an orange cheese stood out remarkably against the scarlet cloth Phyllis had chosen.

'Ouch,' said Angela, closing her eyes.

'It's lovely,' said Rose, overriding her. 'Plebeian but sound.'

Phyllis put a bottle of brown sauce on the table, because Gomer wouldn't eat meat without it, and Rose was less pleased; she hadn't meant to go this far. She had avoided all suggestion of gentle food, but had aimed at a traditional farmhouse meal.

'Oh look,' said Angela, tickled, 'Oh, *really*, Rose.'

Phyllis was unperturbed. She never listened to what they said, unless it concerned Gomer.

Gomer and Jack appeared, clad in immaculate white.

'How smart,' said Angela acidly. 'You put us all to shame.'

141

Jack smiled complacently and took up his plate, seeming quite relaxed despite Michael's efforts to put him at his ease. Even Gomer kept his mouth closed while it was full and spilt only a little beetroot juice on his shirt. His *nain* licked it vigorously before dabbing at it with the dishcloth.

Ermyn stood by the kitchen range. She was too warm there, but she was well away from Gomer.

'Is there any more ham?' asked Michael.

'No,' said Phyllis before Rose could speak. She stood in front of the charger and pushed it away up the table. 'Sandwiches,' she amended, as there was still a considerable quantity.

Michael was taken aback. He put his plate down a little awkwardly. 'Quite right,' he said. 'We mustn't eat too much. Phyllis always knows best.'

Ermyn fidgeted, wondering why Phyllis disliked Michael. For a long time now whenever Michael was home she had grown difficult more often. An egg cracked in the boiling – that would be for Michael. The stale face of the loaf would be his portion if Phyllis had the management of it. Too busy to finish making the beds – and Michael's would be left in its fusty tumble of sheets.

Ermyn knew well the capacity of the Welsh female for taking offence – little girls weeping stonily because someone hadn't offered them a biscuit or had criticised their curls; the village women who lived next door to each other and hadn't spoken for a lifetime; those who went to Llandudno to have their hair done because the hairdresser, who ran the dancing class, hadn't put Myfanwy in the front line of the chorus . . . Perhaps when Gomer was a baby, lying in his pram while his *nain* did the

142

cleaning, lying on his back, little eyes closed, little mouth open – perhaps Michael, home for the holidays with the smooth conscienceless face of boyhood bent on experiment, had dropped in a worm dirty from the garden, glistening and burst, bits of gravel adhering to it. Phyllis would never forgive that. Or perhaps it was just that she wished Gomer could go away to school too, in a cap and socks up to his knees, with a tuckbox. Or perhaps she wished he could have a nice house in London and a pretty wife and lots of money. Or perhaps it was something else . . .

'Ermyn, you're day-dreaming. Help us get the table cleared and we'll go.'

But Ermyn wanted to bring reconciliation and peace to the household, as Rose had brought order and comfort. Perhaps they could work together . . . She smiled at Phyllis idiotically.

'That was very good,' said Henry to his capable wife.

'Delicious,' agreed Edward, clinging determinedly to a bottle of lager Henry had tried to put aside. He looked ill but was quite steady.

There was a slight stir when Michael realised he hadn't brought his cricket boots. Angela said ill-temperedly that when she'd packed she'd been thinking of his father and not his feet, and Michael looked hurt; but Ermyn went hurriedly to the chest in the hall and found an old pair of the Captain's. They were a little worn but would serve. Michael left off his silly hat and put on a pair of rimless sunglasses of the kind favoured by terrorists and assassins and fashionable in London; they made him look like a partially-sighted person. Angela donned a large straw sun hat and waited so that she could walk with Edward,

143

and Phyllis passed Gomer a slice of ham and a pickled onion to eat in his fingers. They went off in good heart.

* * *

Rose and Ermyn returned to the field through the hedge. The players had to make a ceremonial entry up the lane from the coast road. At its opening was a notice inscribed *Llwybr Cyhoeddus* – the other side, that said Public Footpath, had been erased – and Jack had stationed a small boy there with another notice announcing simply 'To the Cricket'.

Angela said they'd better be careful, or the Welsh Nats would be along with a pot of red paint because it wasn't in Welsh. She got so bored with all this silly Nationalism . . .

Bevan the Sweet Shop had set up a trestle table for the purveying of rock, soft drinks and crisps. The other shopkeepers were envious of his enterprise. 'That old Bevan,' they said bitterly. 'Dirty old money-grubber.' The Captain wouldn't have permitted it.

Rose leaned idly against the pavilion. She wore a coat and skirt of linen checked in black and red, black knee-length stockings and a black silk scarf otiose against her black silk hair. Beneath it dangled her grannie's green glass earrings, and she looked brave and strange like a fragile but untrustworthy pirate. Last year she had worn an airy wind-borne chiffon and the twins had danced around her like lambs around their dam. They had offered the plates of sausage rolls and eccles cakes with their own little hands, so delicate and fine they felt like broken toothpicks in little silk bags. The twins had such lovely manners that people who weren't used to them thought they must be joking. 'Show off,' said the locals. 'As if that Rose had anything to swank about.'

Rose tenderly put the twins out of her mind. She hadn't even telephoned them, in case demons waited on the wires for a clue to their whereabouts. She stood up, straight and self-contained, lest her bearing should remind any passing elemental of the lovely absent children and send him seeking them.

Beside her, Ermyn gazed out to sea. Although calm, it did not look reassuring – smooth and wrinkle-free like the face of a saint or a psychopath. She would not have been surprised to hear the newsagent crying the death of God from his yacht in the bay, as another helmsman had once cried over the still water the death of Great Pan. Horror, thought Ermyn: death and anger and horror. She was back in Judges 19 and the dreadful country of the Benjamites, wondering wholly against her will how the Levite had jointed his concubine – with what affronted, legalistic skill he had made her into *twelve* pieces: one each for each of the tribes of Israel. They must have been surprised when they opened the post, she thought mirthlessly, having lost some faith in the disinfecting properties of humour. People didn't cut up naturally into *twelve* pieces. Eleven pieces was what people would cut up into. If the Levite had had a mind inclined to symmetry, and she was sure he had from what she knew of him, it would have annoyed him, the tiresome inability of the human body to fall into twelve even pieces.

Elys Water was gurgling beyond the field. There would be drowned things in it, exposed by the ebbing tide, and the seagulls would be ripping them up. Ermyn gazed surprised at a group of people laughing and talking on her

145

right as though the Elysian Field was a pleasant place – as though the world was a pleasant place. 'I wish the match was over,' she said.

'We won't *watch* it,' said Rose. 'When they're playing we'll go back in the garden.'

* * *

There were quite a few people gathering now. They looked hopelessly inconclusive, like pieces from different games. Players stood around self-consciously hitting their toes with their cricket bats, and spectators sat down carefully on the harsh grass. Virginia Woolf idled around the edges, her yellow devil's eyes unblinking. Some young local girls had precisely the same air, bold but wary. They huddled together, occasionally laughing, loudly but without conviction. A few of the kinder, more motherly landladies had brought their visitors to have a look at the family, obviously hoping that some of their odder friends would be present to make it a real treat. Edward shouldn't disappoint them, thought Rose. He was practising bowling and looked quite mad.

'Perhaps we should stand on our hands and wave our legs in the air,' said Angela, smiling irritably as she became aware of the expectant aspect of some of the watchers. 'Do come here and sit down, Edward. You were up so late. Save your energy for the match.' She drew his arm through hers and led him to the pavilion steps, screening him with her wide pleated skirt, her hat and her expensive scent.

Michael looked nervous. He juggled a little with his bat and did a few dance steps. It was extraordinary how

146

much it mattered to them, thought Rose. They didn't so much want their side to win, though they would never admit it, as to make the most runs themselves and be the hero of the hour, carried shoulder-high to the pavilion. Well, that was the spirit that won the Empire – seeming team-spirit combined with hidden but ruthless self-interest. No wonder cricket was the national sport.

Phyllis stepped out of the pavilion. 'There's some of them black,' she said without emphasis.

'Well, we don't mind if they're pink with green spots, as long as they enjoy cricket, do we?' said Michael behind her. Though not religious, he was not without a uniquely Anglican type of tolerance.

'You know, Phyllis,' said Angela, 'the West Indians and Pakistanis are frightfully good at cricket.'

Nevertheless everyone was relieved the Captain wasn't here. One of the family had been among the first to enter Cawnpore after the massacre, and a certain feeling had lingered on, giving added weight to their natural feelings of racial superiority.

'Cooee, Rose,' said a voice.

'Pauline,' said Rose, pleased, and spinning round. She enjoyed the company of the barmaid from The Goat.

But the barmaid from The Goat was not alone. It seemed that this year she had chosen to lend her allegiance to the visiting team. Last year she had minded Jack's jumper and brought him bottles of lemonade and crisps at regular intervals. Now she was with a large stranger who wore a scarf tucked into his white open-necked shirt. She had her poodle under one arm and was dressed in a pink-and-turquoise Welsh tapestry trouser suit, with a little peaked hat to match.

147

'*Hullo*, Rose,' she said excitedly, not so much out of friendship as to show her companion she was on terms with the toffs. Rose was disappointed in her. 'And Ermyn, you *have* got big.'

'Hullo,' said Ermyn awkwardly, looking at the grass. Pauline had had an unfortunate experience earlier in the year. A commercial traveller had assaulted her and fled, and she had been so upset everyone had been alarmed. The police did nothing and she grew so angry they feared she'd make herself ill. 'Silly girl,' Father had said uneasily, unable to see what all the fuss was about. She'd slept with just about everyone from here to Holyhead, and while perhaps the man should have asked first, surely no real harm had been done. Father, like the English judiciary, found it difficult to discern real evil in any male hetero-sexual activity. He thought the barmaid from The Goat had behaved in an uncharacteristically unsportsmanlike fashion. Moreover, she could have got the commercial traveller into a lot of trouble, going on like that . . . Rose said Father's reaction was an interesting manifestation of a peculiar human phenomenon – the angry bafflement of the conqueror at the ingratitude of the conquered. She had observed it before in various other contexts, she said . . . Like foxes, thought Ermyn, or pheasants – lucky to be singled out for attention by the lords of creation . . . Rose said it was enough to make the stoutest tart tremble.

'. . . London?' said Pauline, for what was plainly the third or fourth time.

'Sorry,' said Ermyn. She faltered and stammered.

'I said – how are you finding London?' repeated Pauline.

'Oh lovely,' said Ermyn. 'Very nice.'

148

'They're a frightfully old family,' Pauline told her companion, refinedly, as they walked away. 'Quite one of the oldest in Wales.'

'You often get that in these old families,' he said wisely. 'It's the inbreeding does it.' He slid his hand round Pauline, under her arm.

'Naughty,' she said. He drew her closer, '. . . why play cricket? . . . a good screw . . .' Ermyn heard him quite clearly. Screws held down coffin lids.

Pauline glanced back at her brightly. 'Shut up,' she said to the man.

'Feels like thunder,' said someone in the pavilion. It had grown hot, but no lighter. Ermyn could feel her feet sweating nervously. This wasn't the place to play cricket. Not this funny field under the mountain, lit with yellow light against which even the white-clad figures looked hard-edged and black. And the people weren't cricketing people, but only pretending. She had seen village cricket, staying with her Hampshire cousins. There had been huge moon-eyed daisies in the long grass and poppies red as pain; they went with the strawberries and the line of elms. And while it was true that as she remembered the sky had slipped a little, hanging too low and at an angle just above the trees, still her relations and their people knew who she was and had no intention of destroying her. She hadn't realised it at the time, but looking back she thought she had probably quite enjoyed that day. There had been very little that was strange about it, and she could fit it into a space in her memory labelled 'village cricket' and be grateful . . . There were few enough events that came up to expectation . . . Unobtrusively, she went back through the hedge and lay down.

'Henry,' said Rose. 'You'd better sit up now, because the opposition seems to be all here.'

Henry groaned but got to his feet.

'Well, well,' said Rose looking closely. A little man in a tam-o'-shanter, his torso naked and streaked like dirty pastry, stood conferring solemnly with Jack. He was clearly the captain of his side.

'It's Ermyn's man,' said Rose. 'She trod on his toe in the village, and he took her for a Cossack horde at least.'

'It'll be a farce,' said Henry.

After a few minutes, when Henry had greeted the man and play had commenced, Rose also backed away to the hedge.

Everyone was behaving very well, clapping and quite often uttering the time-honoured words and sounds appropriate to cricket. Already there were even gasps and sighs. The visitors could scarcely be distinguished from the villagers, and all was muted and polite.

Far away across the field stood Phyllis, dressed as the other women used to dress for chapel, in a flowered nylon dress begrudgingly draped and pleated over her chest, white gloves, shoes and handbag, and a purple felt hat. There was something in her stance that led Rose to believe she understood the rules of the game.

The vicar stood at Silly Point, his legs apart and bent, and his hands stretched, clawlike.

Rose looked round rapidly. Peggy *parchedig* would be hurt at not being asked to lunch and would be determined to come back for drinks, since both she and the vicar were convinced that the family were C of E and that there was a mystic link between this institution and the squire – which was how they saw the Captain. The vicar had a hard time in Llanelys, with his modern views, weak chin and common English accent.

Rose went through the hedge, followed by the claps and loud communal sighs from the pitch. Ermyn was asleep on her back, and Lilliputian insects were considering how best to break her up and carry her away. Rose trod on a beetle for fun and went for a walk round the perimeter.

Ermyn stirred. She felt as though she'd been asleep for years – soaked, sodden, half-drowned in sleep. She could see a noise inside her head: a seagull's cry. Sound transmuted into sight, it trailed across the sky obscenely looped and whirled: the cry of a carrion eater. Two ladybirds crept over her leg, looking like drops of plaguey, independent blood, black-spotted and free from the laws of gravity. Perhaps they'd sneaked out of her veins and were trying to get away and soon a flood would follow . . .

'Ermyn,' she heard. They were looking for her. She crawled forward obediently and stared through the branches. Angela was guiding a large slow figure in dove-grey silk towards her.

'Hullo, dear,' said Lady Watcyn Hogge, peering at her through the leaves.

'Where's Rose?' asked Angela, looking up and down as though Rose were a squirrel. 'Ursula wants to see her.' She sounded incredulous.

Ermyn glanced sideways. Farther down, where the hedge widened into a small thicket, was a dying alder, its low branches fabulously bowed and twisted, snowed over

151

with lichen, eerily green. Rose stood in its indifferent embrace, a finger to her lips.

'She's there,' said Ermyn hopelessly.

Rose stamped ineffectually on the mouldering earth, but she came forward.

'How lovely to see you,' she said, pinching Ermyn on the arm. 'I'll come through.' The hedge was suddenly stiffly hostile, as though it had had enough of this to-ing and fro-ing. It ripped Rose's jacket spitefully. 'Look,' she said. 'A hedge tear.'

'Oh dear, dear,' said Lady Watcyn Hogge. 'I expect it will mend.'

Rose looked beyond her.

'I brought my young people,' said Lady Watcyn Hogge. 'They're very fond of cricket. Say hullo, Christopher.'

'How do you do,' said the banana-smeared young man of the party and Ermyn's two school friends. They didn't look fond of cricket. They looked bored.

Ermyn felt hunted.

Rose was annoyed. Had she known that the *bonheddigion*, the gentry, were coming, she would have planned accordingly – an Edwardian tea on the lawn, white cloths and the Crown Derby to frighten Angela, or a thirties tea on the terrace with a cake disguised as a tiny cricket pitch and little rolled sandwiches with flags describing their contents. They would never see the point of the tea in the pavilion.

As she was thinking this and pretending to listen to Ursula, who was speaking, the bishop's wife joined them. Peggy *parchedig* followed, talking animatedly and waving her hands.

Virginia Woolf wandered by, her lower jaw rotating.

'Oh, there you are, Bea,' said Ursula to the bishop's wife. 'I thought we'd lost you.'

'. . . bishop?' Rose asked.

'Oh, he couldn't come, my dear,' said the bishop's wife fervently, pressing Rose's arm. 'He was *so* disappointed.'

'It's a splendid game,' said Lady Watcyn Hogge. She clapped as a shout arose from the other side of the field.

Rose took the opportunity to question Ermyn, drawing her aside.

Ermyn shook her head. 'It was Angela,' she whispered. 'She asked them all at the party. I thought you knew.'

'Something's happened,' said Angela. Across the field a flowered, white-tipped figure bent over someone clothed in white, scarlet-haired and prone.

Ermyn turned away. She would never have made a nurse, even if Father hadn't almost choked at the mere suggestion. Her instinct when something was hurt in her presence was to shut her ears or its screaming mouth. Death was better than pain.

The figures rose and parted. Rose caught sight of Michael. He seemed to be explaining something.

'Come into the garden,' said Rose. 'It's more sheltered.'

A wind was following Elys Water as the tide turned, and Rose wanted to consider for a moment the situation when these ladies should mingle with the teams and decide whether there was any amusement or profit to be gained from it.

Christopher held back the branches for his aunt and the bishop's wife. They were followed by Angela, Peggy *parchedig*, Ermyn and, finally, the girls. As the second girl went through, he let go of a supple twig, which must have stung quite painfully as it sprang against her. She swung round and hissed at him.

'I'll get you for that,' she said giggling, and throwing a handful of leaves at his face.

Rose was depressed. They were too stupid to bother with at all.

'How pleasant this is,' said the bishop's wife to Ermyn. 'I remember when your mother was alive we used to have some splendid parties here.'

'Oh, there are still parties,' said Peggy *parchedig*. 'The Captain lets us have our garden fête here for the church.'

'How kind,' said the bishop's wife remotely.

It was odd, thought Ermyn, how much more at home were the bishop and his wife with their own class than with their clergy.

'We're not having them any more,' said Rose. 'Those ghastly kids kick up the lawn.'

'Oh, they do,' agreed Ursula, 'and it takes such years to get a lawn just so.'

Ermyn felt sorry for Peggy. She had on her best frock, and clean ankle socks. Like many very plain girls she believed that a woman's crowning glory, if given enough rein, would make up for her deficiencies. She had done her hair in a single plait which hung over her left shoulder and down her front. The effect of this combined with her flat-heeled shoes was quite infuriating, and people other than Rose were already beginning to stare and mutter acrimoniously.

'Come and see the hens,' said Ermyn. 'They're so pretty. Rose chose them.'

'You go too,' said Ursula to her nephew and the girls.

They went, but not after Ermyn.

Soon the high-pitched sounds of privileged youth at play drifted from the upper lawn.

'I hope they don't disturb the Captain,' said Ursula.

'Nothing disturbs him,' said Rose, glad to be rid of the young people.

'Come and see the garden,' said Angela to the two ladies, and she described to them the current triumphs and backslidings of the rhododendrons and roses.

'Pssst,' said a voice.

'Oh, it's you,' said Rose, as Pauline parted the branches and beckoned to her. 'I'm ashamed of you.'

'He *is* a randy thing,' admitted Pauline readily, 'but he's in a very nice line of business.' She cuddled her poodle.

'You have terrible taste,' said Rose. As she climbed again through the hedge her silk scarf caught and pulled askew. She decided that she would introduce Pauline to the ladies when there was a nice clear space in the afternoon. Would she say, 'Pauline, this is Ursula and Bea. The barmaid from The Goat', which would discomfit them. Or would she say, 'Pauline, do you know Lady Watcyn Hogge and Mrs Flower, the wife of the bishop, you know – ', which would discomfit Pauline. Imagining the paralysis of gentility that would descend on her, Rose smiled remorselessly.

'What are you laughing at?' asked Pauline suspiciously, twisting round to see if she had torn her trouser suit.

'Nothing,' said Rose. 'That's a terrible get-up you've got on,' she added, compelled by her aesthetic sense, as occasionally happened, to speak the truth.

155

'It's real Welsh tapestry,' said Pauline astonished, obviously putting this native cloth in the same high class as Harris tweed, or Thai silk.

'I don't care if it's Bayeux tapestry,' said Rose. 'It's horrid.'

'Well, it would be a very dull world if we all had the same taste,' said Pauline offendedly. She went on stroking her poodle and looked, with exaggerated interest, at the game. 'Your friend's doing well,' she observed. 'The small fellow in the glasses. I believe that was a six.'

Rose allowed her the point. Pauline was, at least, not stupid. She sat down, calling a truce. 'He won't keep it up,' she confided. 'I've poisoned him.'

'You're the devil, Rose,' said Pauline placidly.

The man in the tam-o'-shanter was bowling with insane determination. A number of his supporters were rhythmically striking soft-drink cans with stones and singing a little song known only to themselves. The other spectators had drawn away from them, and Edward didn't like the noise. He shrugged at the undertaker, who was umpiring, and pointed his bat at the sky; but he was too well-schooled to protest more vigorously and carried on. The undertaker was English and biased. His daughter had married a doctor from Manchester and had a German au pair for her children, but Rose had never asked them up to the *Plâs*. Who does she think she is, he was wont to ask, rhetorically.

Edward was pale and greasy with weariness, and his strokes lacked resolution.

'He does look tired,' said a voice behind Rose. They had all come back from the garden to encourage the home team, or perhaps for their tea.

156

'You know who he *is*, don't you?' said Ursula to the bishop's wife.

'Of course,' she answered. 'I think he writes so beautifully. Such a rarity in these days.'

'Your sister-in-law's holding his cardie.' Pauline, always alert to erotic significance, nudged Rose suggestively.

'She fancies him,' said Rose.

'Then she must be pretty hard up,' said Pauline.

They gossiped in whispers, sitting on the ground, while the party standing behind them murmured and clapped.

*　　*　　*

Ermyn, the scales fallen from her eyes, watched in silence. It was perfectly clear to her what was going on. Hostility was concentrated in the small ball hurtling over the field to maim the soft and brittle guardian of the wicket. They had given him a bat in a show of fair play, but Ermyn knew that everyone wished he would put it away and honestly, sincerely, protect those bits of wood with his flesh alone – his person. Why else throw the thing at him with such physical intensity?

'Oh,' said everyone. They clapped, hooted, rose, turned, stretched their legs, or ran forward. The match was over.

'Who won?' Rose asked Henry. She was fairly certain, but she had no way of knowing and wanted reassurance.

'*They* did,' said Henry.

'My poor *darling*,' said Rose, delighted. She reached up to kiss his neck. It was dry, and mavellously warm in the gloomy field, and she felt a momentary sorrow. 'I love you,' she said. Ermyn, overhearing, did not believe her.

Rose slid her slim, cold shoulder under Henry's arm

and bent her elbow against his waist and they walked, in step, to the pavilion.

'The game's the thing,' said the bishop's wife.

In the hut people were already jostling for sandwiches. Triumph and despondency curdled in the air. The young people were in the forefront. 'Have a paste *butty*,' they cried hilariously. '*You* have one,' said the bigger girl, pushing a slimy bit of bread down Christopher's shirt.

'High spirits,' said Lady Watcyn Hogge, a little dismayed.

They were beyond Rose's competence, insulated by naïveté, safe from all her wit. She hoped the fish paste had gone off.

Tam-o'-shanter stood among the loud crowd of admirers, his expression serious and unsurprised. Rose recognised it – it came from complete assurance.

Gomer, pale and sullen, sat on a folding stool, his friends around him like a wedding group, and his grandmother hovering, untypically doubtful. His father had somehow managed to identify with the winning team and glanced backwards at his sulking child with rather more contempt than concern.

Phyllis looked like Gomer, past comfort or jest. It was plain she wasn't going to make the tea.

'What upset Gomer?' asked Rose. His colds, bruises, diarrhoea had cost her many hours of Phyllis's working time.

'He would have made the highest score, but Michael, who was in with him, gave him the wrong call from the other end and ran him out,' said Henry distantly.

'Came a hell of a crump,' said a Midlands voice with great satisfaction.

'This is frightfully good,' said the bishop's wife earnestly, of a sandwich.

'Well, only Phyllis can work the urn, and now she won't,' said Rose, growing dangerously bored with the scene.

'I'll do it,' said Lady Watcyn Hogge, whose ancestors had behaved with decision and aplomb all through the heyday of the British Empire. 'That's pretty,' she said to Angela, looking at the flower arrangement. 'Did you do it, dear?'

No one liked the tea. 'Water bewitched,' said one. 'Gnat's piss,' said another.

Rose led the way out of the hut, and sat down.

'Have you thought any more about ecumenism?' Mrs Flower asked Ermyn.

'Oh yes. Thank you,' said Ermyn. 'What *is* ecumenism?' she asked Rose in an undertone.

'It is as though a dying man were to tie himself to one already dead in the hope of setting in train a process of revitalisation,' Rose told her, also in an undertone, low but carrying.

'It's lovely,' gabbled Peggy *parchedig*. 'Charlie went to talk to the nuns the other day. They were lovely to him. And the Father gave us a sermon at Easter. It was lovely.'

'How lovely,' said Rose, leaning back on her elbows. 'If the progressives in my poor befuddled Church have their way,' she said to Ermyn, 'thousands more clergymen's wives will be unleashed on to the world. Ponder that, if ever you feel overwhelmed by unreasoning cheerfulness.'

Ermyn giggled guiltily. She didn't care if Rose *was* a terrorist, a secret deadly fighter . . . She stopped giggling suddenly. That was not a thought she had intended to

159

think and she didn't know where it had come from, nor did she like it.

'Celibacy is dreadfully unhealthy,' said Angela with a backward, censorious glance. 'Unnatural.'

'I have never had much time for nature,' said Rose.

The lust of the eyes, the lust of the flesh and the pride of life, thought Ermyn.

'That's why I always say protestantism is such a *sensible* religion,' said Angela, with a kindly approving nod to the bishop's wife.

'Sensible religion is a contradiction in terms,' said Rose. 'Protestantism isn't a religion at all. It has merely elevated all the minor vices and weaknesses into major virtues – meanness and anal preoccupations into thrift and cleanliness, clannishness into respectability, xenophobia into loyalty. Concupiscence is justified by marriage, and arrogance by the claim that the Lord loves them. They justify their lack of culture, visual sense and imagination by decrying adornment, and they make up all those explicit flat-footed hymns because they have no feeling for the numinous – no belief in God, in fact.'

Even Ermyn thought this was rude, but nobody took any notice.

Virginia Woolf ambled past, eating a sausage roll.

'Little lamb, who made thee?' queried Angela. 'Dost thou know who made thee?'

Pauline muttered something coarse about the ram in the field behind them and giggled.

'Have you met the bishop's wife?' asked Rose affectionately.

'So sweet,' said Mrs Flower. 'So tame. How do you do.'

'I adore Blake,' said Ursula to Angela. 'Blake and

160

Betjeman, my favourites . . . And Tolkien, of course.'

'Have you seen the Muppet Show?' asked Rose.

Ermyn was surprised at Virginia Woolf's appearance. For a moment she didn't recognise her. All the sheep had been fleeced and looked frail and rather ill. The merry, pipe-cleaner lambs of the spring – crying to their mothers in their perfect French, *mère, mère* – had sobered into these thin, apprehensive creatures already out of place in the green fields. Their background now should be the sterile white, the mean grey metal of the slaughter-house. Bitterly she regretted her joke about consuming legs and shoulders. It was Death who was the joker – all the joy of life ended up teased and misled to the grave and the stench that was the end of everything. Eaten and dead. Worms, thought Ermyn: worms and murder and death. No one had ever succeeded in wiping the smile off Death's head.

'They look just like people in dirty combinations, now they've had their woolly overcoats taken off,' said Angela whimsically.

The vicar emerged from the hut. 'Quite a jolly party,' he remarked uncertainly. He knew he wasn't popular, and in the absence of a congregation he had begun to devote his energies to a movement towards a clergymen's union – they were shamefully underpaid.

In the hut the sounds were increasing in volume and frequency, the voices of the young people audible above the rest. 'Oh, you beast. Just wait till I get you. Take that.' They weren't mixing, but playing out between themselves their irresolute, dissatisfied sexual game.

The lower classes too had settled into a tribal rhythm. 'I wish I was a fascinating bitch –' sang an ageing voice.

161

'They're not getting like that on the tea,' said Rose.

'Edward contributed a case of beer,' said Henry. 'Good of him.'

'We must get back to the boozer in Dirty Filthy,' yelled someone, screeching with laughter at this rendering of the name of the hamlet adjacent to Llanelys. 'We've ordered our dinner.'

'Denis says he doesn't know how they can afford it,' said Peggy timorously. 'We can never afford to eat out.'

'I can tell you,' said Angela grimly. 'Michael's taxes. Those of us who work hard are simply subsidising the rest.'

A cricket ball ricocheted against the wooden walls, and a Midlander rolled backwards down the steps.

'People like that get awfully silly on drink,' said Angela. 'Mummy never allowed it when we had fêtes and things at home.' She realised Edward would soon be drunk again and was annoyed with him.

'. . . I'd sleep all day and work all night,' carolled the ladies in the hut.

The more sedate onlookers were already leaving the field. Middle-aged women collected their husbands and led them away. As they passed Rose and Henry they nodded formally. 'Very good game,' they said. 'A very good game.'

A pair of itinerant Americans approached. They were recognisable by the convenient light-weight, drip-dry clothes in sensible, neutral colours that they wore, and by the eagerness with which they advanced to seek enlightenment.

'Was that *cricket*?' asked the female in ringing tones.

'Yes,' said Henry, doubtfully.

162

'It was cricket,' she explained to her husband.

He took a photograph of them all, after first asking Ursula's permission, and they moved on, their air of bewildered affability intact, in search of other quaint local customs.

'What a pity Edward missed that,' said Rose. 'He likes Americans.' Edward thought that now Great Britain had been betrayed and emasculated by the greed and sloth of the working classes America was the last bastion of civilisation in a world ever increasingly favouring the Left like a bird with a crippled wing.

'They're so friendly, aren't they?' said Mrs Flower. 'Such delightful manners.'

'And how rare that is,' said Angela, as yet another Midlander emerged from the hut and trod on her hand without a word of apology. 'I have absolutely no patience with all these women's libbers.' She edged further away from the steps. 'I like having doors opened for me, and being helped on with my coat, and being treated like a *woman.*'

'Of course,' said the bishop's wife. 'I always say, if God had meant us all to be the same he'd have made us the same.'

'A lot of them are lesbians, you know,' said Angela seriously.

'Poor things,' said the bishop's wife. 'I expect they feel they've got to keep their end up.'

Pauline suddenly snorted.

'Something go down the wrong way?' asked the bishop's wife with cold concern.

'She suffers from epilepsy,' Rose whispered. '*Grand mal.*'

'Oh, poor thing,' said Mrs Flower, suddenly turning on Pauline with a smile of nervous but Christian compunction. 'They have such marvellous drugs today,' she said.

Pauline shrank back, startled.

'I *must* go,' said the bishop's wife hurriedly. 'Sunday tomorrow. Not a day of rest for us wives of the clergy, you know!'

'What's *she* been drinking?' asked Pauline *sotto voce*.

'The milk of human kindness,' said Rose. 'Goodbye, Mrs Flower. It was good of you to come.'

'She looks as though *it's* gone down the wrong way,' said Pauline resentfully. 'Hope she chokes. Does she think I'm a junkie or something?'

'She's always been eccentric,' explained Rose, 'and she has a hard time being married to the bishop. He . . .' she lowered her voice.

'The *poor* thing,' said Pauline, who being an Irish Catholic of the old school like Rose was prepared to believe anything of a Protestant.

'I must go too,' said Peggy *parchedig*. 'Sunday tomorrow – ' She paused expectantly, and after a moment added: 'Goodbye. It's been a lovely day, Rose.'

The back of Ermyn's nose began to ache. Through tears as stinging as soapy water she watched the small ungainly figure walking away. She despised her own cravenness. If Rose hadn't been there, she'd have gone after Peggy *parchedig*, taken her arm, told her she *couldn't* go, the evening would fail without her . . . Then, with debilitating honesty, she admitted that it wasn't Rose, it was her own reluctance to be associated with such piteous unattractiveness that kept her where she

164

was. But as Peggy disappeared down the lane Ermyn almost got to her feet.

'Sit down,' said Rose.

'I should go too,' said Ursula, but her voice lacked conviction. It was plain the young people would not be easily rounded up.

'But you *must* stay to supper,' cried Angela, speaking as a daughter of the house. 'It simply won't be the same without *any* of Father's old friends.'

'Well, it *would* be nice,' said Ursula. 'I'll just go and tell the children.'

On her way up the steps of the hut she collided with Pauline's friend who was coming down. He ignored her, crying, 'Where is she then? Where are you, gorgeous?'

'I'm here,' said Pauline, rising with splendid confidence. They walked away across the field entwined, quite of one mind, the little dog following.

Rose started back to the house. As she went she could hear Michael speaking in an assumed Birmingham accent. A Midlander was returning the compliment: 'Ai say, eeold freeuit – '

A reluctant smile settled like a butterfly on Rose's small scarlet-painted mouth.

＊　　　＊　　　＊

The house was quite silent except for the kitchen clock tick-ticking, sewing up the unpleasant day with neat, steady stitches. Blod had gone. The quality of emptiness was unmistakable. Rose would never have trusted her to sit with the twins. The doctor had been: a disposable hypodermic syringe lay reproachfully on the dresser. Jack hadn't asked him to play. Too old, he'd said. And no bloody good.

Perhaps the Captain had died. Whatever his condition, there was nothing Rose could do to ease it. She would pretend she thought Blod was still with him.

Her own parents had died decorously, uninsistently, as though loth to give her any trouble. Even her father, who had never apologised for anything, had gone quietly.

She began to assemble the supper.

Ermyn ran breathlessly up the lawn. 'Oh Rose,' she called at the drawing-room window. 'Rose,' she cried at the drawing-room door.

'What the hell?' asked Rose, peering into the passage.

'Oh Rose,' said Ermyn. 'The barmaid from The Goat's dog is chasing Virginia Woolf. She's in an awful state. They've gone into the bushes and she says they'll go down on to the road and be killed.'

'I don't care what they do,' said Rose, 'as long as they do it quietly.'

'But Rose,' said Ermyn, stopping to catch her breath. 'It *is* getting a bit out of hand. They're trying to move the pavilion and there are some men with beards and *Plaid Cymru* T-shirts . . .'

'They'll be from Wolverhampton,' said Rose. 'I don't imagine a lot of dangerous political activists would go charging about with their persuasions blazoned on their chests. They get those shirts from the newsagents. They think it's a scream.'

Ermyn sat down, incapable of conveying to Rose the sense of violent and dangerous frivolity that seemed to possess everyone left in the Elysian Field. Perhaps it was her imagination.

166

Uncharacteristically Rose poured herself a whisky and knelt to light the drawing-room fire on the north wall. The kindling crackled crossly until the logs caught and the flames sprang up the chimney. 'It *has* been a terrible day,' she admitted, as her hands warmed.

Lady Watcyn Hogge and Angela coming through the french windows were not sufficiently recovered to deny this.

'They just won't go,' said Angela. 'They're absolutely settled in.'

'St Peter got rid of the Welshmen in Heaven by making an angel stand outside and yell Toasted Cheese,' said Rose.

'Oh, don't be stupid, Rose,' said Angela. 'Most of them aren't even Welsh.'

'Try Fire,' suggested Rose, 'or Free Love, or Drinks on the House in The Goat.'

'They'll be all right,' said Ursula. 'Just a little horse play.' She spoke calmly, but she was no longer tidy. There was a smear of margarine down the shoulder of her dress and some leaves and small things in her hair. She seemed unaware of them.

'That settles it,' said Henry, stalking in decisively. 'That's the very last year.' He threw his bat down on the sofa and sat on it. 'They've shifted the hut half off its supports and I caught one of them starting a bonfire.'

'What did you do?' asked Rose.

'I trod on it,' said Henry.

All the women looked at his feet resting on the Chinese silk rug.

Edward crept in like a bad dog and lurked, disgraced but hopeful, by the walnut table where the drinks stood.

167

'Did you get to Glyndebourne this year?' asked Angela of Ursula, as no one else was speaking.

'*I* did,' said Edward unexpectedly, with sudden enthusiasm. 'I went with . . .' He mentioned two of his dear friends, a big frisky opera singer and her droll, constipated husband, a concert pianist.

Angela forgave him immediately. 'Oh, how lovely,' she cried. 'I do admire her so.'

'You must meet them,' said Edward. 'You must come to dinner when I get back.' He eyed the whisky.

'You haven't got a drink,' said Angela, getting up and pouring him one.

'Where's Michael?' asked Ermyn.

'I'm hungry,' said Henry. 'I didn't get any tea.'

'I'm just going to see to supper,' said Rose, who was beginning to feel sleepy. The firelight shone on Henry's dirty shoes and the short golden hairs on his arms and his high broad cheekbones.

'We'll come and help,' said Ursula, 'and the men can have their post mortem in peace.'

'Shirlee, Shirlee . . .' came a distant demented wail. Pauline was still seeking her poodle. Angela was glad – Rose was quite capable of asking her back to supper.

Phyllis was in the kitchen. She had put on her flowered overall but had retained her hat and white shoes.

'Did you enjoy the game?' asked Angela.

'Nrgg,' said Phyllis, tight-toothed, clashing cutlery.

Suddenly, astonishingly, she began to laugh, putting her head back and showing her false teeth right down to the hinges of her jaw. She supported herself on the dresser, bent her legs, slapped her thigh. The others stood

168

smiling uncertainly in the presence of this exclusive mirth.

'What's so funny?' asked Rose.

Phyllis stopped laughing and looked round furtively.

Angela and Ursula hurriedly turned away and began to talk.

Phyllis beckoned. 'Did you see that old Michael? They pushed him over, right in a dirty old cow pat.'

'No,' said Rose. 'I didn't see that. I heard he'd run Gomer out.'

Phyllis stopped laughing. '*Ar Michael Diawl yna,*' she said with such ferocity that even Rose was taken aback. The words spat and leapt like angry startled cats or the fat in the fire, uncontrollable, brief, dispersed. Phyllis composed herself. 'I'll be getting upstairs,' she said colourlessly, drying her hands on her overall as she went.

'She's mad,' said Ermyn involuntarily.

'You're as bad as Rose,' said Angela turning. 'You both exaggerate so.'

Ermyn reflected that it was either madness or an extraordinary strength of character that enabled people to switch emotions so suddenly. Perhaps they were the same thing. Her own psychic landscape remained the same. Sometimes the sun shone, but mostly it rained. Always the landmarks were there, to be avoided as much as possible but a reminder of the nature of the terrain. It was bad to see things clearly. Ermyn pined after the innocence of optimism, the milkiness of hope – light in the eyes, obscuring mists. Even rage was good and natural: a storm might change things, sweep things away. She would go on a journey, outwards, not to be tormented. She would not stay to have things shown to her. Swinging round resolutely, she put her fingers in the butter.

169

'Do look what you're doing, darling,' said Angela.

The kitchen was full of women doing things the wrong way. Rose took the loaf which Ursula had placed on the chopping board, put it back in the bread crock and brought out the warmed rolls from the oven, placing them on the bread board. Skilfully she slid the charger of chicken from underneath Angela's industrious claws and covered it in a creamy dressing, leaving the neat slices of breast unmixed with the darker, tattier meat of the legs.

Jack the Liar looked in for a moment. 'Want anything? Good game. Good evening, ladies,' he said, hastily retiring as he realised there would be no pickings yet.

'You're so lucky to keep your gardener,' said Ursula to Angela, although they all knew she had two part-time ones of her own.

'It's Father,' said Angela. 'They're incredibly loyal.'

In the drawing-room spirits were lifting with drink and the expectation of food.

'I wouldn't have dropped that catch,' said Michael, dishevelled, and lately arrived, catching up on the whisky. 'Only those damned shoes were slippery as glass. Father must have had them since school.' He sat down to gaze into the fire, his knees bent and his arms around them. 'They'll change their tune,' he said with seeming irrelevance, 'when unemployment really begins to bite.'

'You might have changed,' said Angela, not extending her reproof to the other two players, and without any pretence at raillery. 'You smell.'

'Only a bit of honest sweat,' said Michael. He sank back into his chair with the stubbornly cheerful unconcern of the bullied husband.

The sounds inseparable from glorious achievement were

170

still audible from the Elysian Field. Someone was shouting 'Onward Christian Soldiers' and there were animal-like howls and occasional laughter. A thin shriek rose above the rest . . . 'Shirlee, Shirlee . . .' Poor Pauline would never rest until she had found her poodle.

'Ai say, old chap,' bellowed a Midlander.

'Christopher, the girls . . .' began Ursula uneasily.

Edward closed the french windows. 'Midges,' he explained.

Rose was eating breast of chicken like a starving cat, her head bent over her plate and her teeth greedily snatching it in. It was her first meal of the day and she had saved the best bits for herself. Ermyn was entranced to see that she still looked beautiful given over to this fleshly pursuit. Her teeth were not, after all, pointed, but round and white, like rice. The others looked disgusting – their necks stretched over their laps, sucking up trailing afterthoughts of sauce and chicken sinew. Seagulls, worms: undiscriminating and voracious.

Ermyn looked at the fire. The food was too delicious not to eat, and when Edward put his plate down she finished her supper. It was only like school after all – if you sat opposite an adenoidal girl who breathed through her mouth even while eating, you just waited until she had stopped and the memory had faded and then ate your own cooling meal. One had to live, after all . . .

After all – thought Ermyn, beginning to relax . . .

* * *

The stone, coinciding, as it did, with the cheese, came as a terrible shock to them all.

171

'Bloody yobs,' said Michael, leaping up and staring at the cutting black space in the grey window.

Ursula gazed bemusedly at a sliver of glass lying peacefully on her plate, spiking her cheese.

'That's it,' said Henry.

'Missa est,' said Rose, merely out of nostalgia.

'Police,' said Edward.

'I *said* we should never have had the match without him,' said Angela.

Henry jumped over the side of the sofa, knocking the whisky to the floor, and flung open the windows. Then he stood quite still, looking from side to side.

The hunting instinct, thought Ermyn.

'They've gone now,' said Rose, stepping in front of him and closing the windows. She had no doubt as to who had done it. It was not the victorious team who rampaged about, wreaking destruction. She remembered Gomer, junket-pale and thwarted – and he hadn't had any supper.

'Leave it to me,' she said, with such composure, gathering up plates as she went, that they all sat down, glaring a little, and muttering, but too tired to argue.

'*Bloody* yobs,' said Michael once more, stretching his legs and folding his hands over his stomach.

'Oh so *naughty*,' said Ursula.

*   *   *

In the kitchen Rose opened the back door. The darkness stirred slightly by the double gates.

'Rose,' came a distant whisper. 'Hullo, Rose.'

Perhaps in his drunken euphoria he thought she had come to comfort him, to laugh with him.

172

'Don't you call me Rose,' said Rose, whispering too, her words as icy and distinct as snowflakes. 'You creepy little bastard.'

The darkness stilled, and Rose closed the door. He knew that she knew, and that should be the end of the matter. She wondered how far he would go before his fatuity outweighed his grandmother's usefulness. He behaved as though he were invincible, as though he had a hold over them . . .

'Bloody boy,' said Rose aloud.

*   *   *

Ursula wanted to go home. She was tired and she had had a shock. 'Christopher,' she said, plaintively. 'The girls.'

'Don't worry,' said Angela, who was also growing tired of people and thinking of more intense, private pursuits. 'Jack can run them home, or they can easily stay here.'

'Such a nuisance,' moaned Ursula. 'Young people . . . Oh, my bag.' She looked around distractedly. 'Now where . . ?'

They searched without enthusiasm and without success in the drawing-room and the kitchen and the hall and the bathroom and even the green bedroom, where Angela craftily led Ursula to see what she'd say, but she said nothing except that she didn't think she'd been in there and where could she have left the wretched thing.

'It must be in the pavilion,' she said at last. 'It doesn't matter. There was nothing in it. I have my keys here.' She cast a finger down the neck of her dress and fished up a thin silver chain with several keys and what looked like a wedding-ring winking and flashing on it.

173

'One of the men will go,' said Angela.

'No, no my dear,' said Ursula determinedly. 'I wouldn't think of it. If you find it, keep it for me.' She jumped thankfully and hastily into her little French hyena-like car and left for her own chaste home.

Henry went to bed. Edward was asleep on the sofa. Michael had disappeared.

'Ermyn,' said Angela. 'Do go down and look in the pavilion. She says there's nothing in it, but, it's real alligator. Italian. Take a torch.'

Ermyn couldn't refuse. She had never learnt how to. 'But . . .' she said, feebly. She had just discovered why she had been feeling so weary, so bloated and unusually inattentive. The onset of menstruation had not been a great shock to her – she had been prepared for it by her headmistress at school, who had taken upon herself the thankless task of warning the previously carefree little girls of this troublesome and unhygienic nuisance. 'It is nature's way of preparing you for motherhood,' she had said, 'a natural function and nothing to fear. You may feel a little sleepy, and possibly even a little depressed, each month, but you can still swim and ride and carry on your normal lives. And of course,' she added, laughing, 'you can still wash your hair, and you *must* bath. You won't get colds.' But no one had been pleased with this evidence of maturity, Ermyn least of all. She hadn't even been pleased to develop breasts. They got in the way of her arms. And she still could never remember her dates, could never understand the tedious cyclic malaise that overwhelmed her. And she hated swimming and riding anyway.

Miserably, she took the torch from the chest in the hall. She had a dragging pain low down between her hips and she longed to go to bed, but she would rather have died than tell Angela – bring upon herself Angela's scented complicity.

Angela sat down by Edward on the sofa and wriggled and sighed until he woke.

*   *   *

Rose kicked a small mushroom box round the kitchen and made herself a cup of strong black coffee. In between sips she said some very evil words. It had been the sort of day her father would have described as all hell in a basket.

Phyllis came down in her dressing-gown to fill hot water bottles. 'Lot of noise before?' she said.

'Some horrible fool threw a stone through the window,' said Rose. 'It was nothing.'

Anyone watching would have thought they were both mad, laughing at a joke they in no way shared, alone in the night-time kitchen.

*   *   *

Ermyn had gone and was coming back the long way round, too nervous to attempt to breach the hedge in the heavy darkness. She clasped Ursula's bag in one hand and her torch in the other. The field had been deserted; the hut was silent and empty, the alligator bag lying untouched beside the urn – it had frightened her a little to think that there were worse villainies than petty larceny afoot tonight.

There were still some people in the lane, visitors. They stood together under the solitary street lamp, men and girls. Ermyn had to push into the hedge to get past, and

175

they watched her with their lowering bovine stare. 'Oh, pardon *me*,' said one as she hurried by, and a girl laughed – a high, unfriendly sound.

The gate in the wall was open and Ermyn hesitated, overcome by real fright – it was always kept closed. She wanted to scream. She could sense people creeping up behind her, and waiting for her, united in a grinning, shadowy conspiracy. She stepped carefully over the slate sill and pushed the gate closed, the unuttered scream lying like an egg in her throat. For relief she could have howled, whirled round and round, shaken her arms at the starless sky, jumped in and out of the bushes of sage and rosemary and lavender, but she walked on decorously and silently. She had turned off her torch – it made the darkness worse; the enemy came in as close as they dared to its blinding beam. Perhaps the *cwn annwn*, the hounds of hell who ranged the lower air, had scented her and were closing in, hungry for blood. Phyllis still feared them. Smiling a little with sly shyness, she bought Gomer blue pyjamas, because that was a colour they hated . . .

At the bend in the path where the hydrangeas began, Ermyn stopped. Someone was whispering, real unimagined whispering.

'Oh, come on,' said a familiar voice, dreadfully tender. 'Oh come on. I didn't mean it.'

Without thought she switched on her torch. 'Shoo,' she said clearly, pretending it was only Virginia Woolf in there, eating the young leaves. 'Shoo, shoo.'

In the sudden appalled silence and the long isosceles beam of the torch she saw Michael leap up, stare round briefly and run awkwardly towards the house. He would be awkward, she thought, with his clothes like that.

The next moment someone seized her round the knees and flung her down into the bushes. For an instant she thought the barmaid from The Goat had gone berserk, unhinged with grief at the loss of her little dog. But they all said Pauline smelt like the inside of a whore's handbag, and her assailant smelt of sweat and sheep and pencils. The village boys had smelt like that when they were teasing her, pulling her hair, snapping her hat elastic . . .

'The act of love,' thought Ermyn madly, plunged without real warning into the country of the Benjamites. There was a fearful inevitability about her situation. She should never have read that story; she should have known better. The Levite's concubine had crawled back to the doorstep, had died there as the day began to spring. It wasn't so late. She bit Gomer's ugly freckled arm with savage determination and hit his nasty knowing eye with her clenched fist. He struggled on with the thoughtlessness of the male spider.

Ermyn was thinking of Michael – how, like Father, he would never allow Gomer into the drawing-room: spotty, stinking stable boy. Such snobbery. She gave herself up to terrified rage. She had never given her body much thought. Part of her – all her internal organs – were situated in a foreign country, far far away. She was an angel, or perhaps a doll. 'I will kill you,' she said to herself, her own hands taking on an unknown metallic strength. 'I'll kill you . . .'

The light sprang on in the long parlour, easing the blackness.

'Stop it, stop it,' someone cried.

Reproved, she eased her grip.

177

'Let her go,' cried Christopher, jumping into the bushes, followed by the girls leaping like maenads and screeching. Nobly, Christopher drew back his manly fist and hit Gomer. Ermyn giggled, he looked so ridiculous and out-of-date: he was playing a part like Rose, but not nearly so well. There was a horrid drowning sound and even in the night she could see the lower half of Gomer's face darkening. He staggered up and ran blindly to the wall.

'Are you all right?' asked Christopher awkwardly.

'Yes, *are* you?' asked the girls in the sudden, embarrassing silence.

'Yes, thank you,' said Ermyn quite calmly. 'He was drunk, of course.'

'Of course,' they agreed.

'These people get awfully silly with drink.'

'Yes, awfully.'

'Would you care for a cup of coffee?' asked Ermyn formally.

'No, no thank you. We must get back – my aunt . . .'

'Your aunt has gone,' said Ermyn. 'The buses have stopped.'

'It's quite all right,' said the girls. 'We found a dear little man in the village who said he'd run us home. He's waiting in The Goat.'

It was probably Jack the Sycophant, thought Ermyn. 'Yes, of course,' she said. 'Well, goodnight.'

'Goodnight.'

'Goodnight.'

'Goodnight.'

'No,' said Ermyn, aloud. '*No.*' The sound went up with the smell of broken sage and sweet herbs into the enclosing night.

She set about clearing the incident from her mind. In the morning Christopher and the girls would realise that Gomer had fallen and she had been trying to help him up. They would realise their mistake and forget about the whole thing. Michael had been bird-watching. He had a passion for bird-watching, and you couldn't watch owls, for instance, by day.

She felt for her torch. It went on quite readily, proving that the whole scene had been greatly exaggerated. As her torch still worked, there could have been no real violence, certainly no blood.

Quite devoid of fear, thinking elaborately, Ermyn went back to the house.

'What was all that yelling and thudding?' asked Rose, as Ermyn entered the kitchen.

'It was Virginia Woolf,' said Ermyn. 'The barmaid from The Goat's dog chased her into the bushes.'

'I thought they'd gone hours ago,' said Rose.

'Oh, no,' said Ermyn.

'I think they've all gone stark staring mad,' said Rose. 'Michael just came in looking as though the hounds of hell were after him.'

'Oh, he was helping,' said Ermyn. 'He had to go right into the bushes.'

'Well, I hope you got them out,' said Rose. 'We don't cultivate the flowers for Michael and the sheep to jump on. You'd better go to bed. You look terrible.'

'It's only the curse,' said Ermyn. 'Goodnight.'

'Goodnight,' said Rose.

'Goodnight.'

*   *   *

Sunday was severely attenuated, dull with a sense of anti-climax. Everyone slept late and retired early. Phyllis spent the day in the sickroom. Little was said.

Rose was cross because the Boys' Brigade had played their trumpets on the way to church, spoiling the clear air. The sound made her think of baked mutton and Welsh boiled cabbage, she said, and ruined her day. It all went to make up the heavy, greasy, pervasive atmosphere of a Welsh Sunday, and Llanelys was in a dry county – though it made no real difference: the drinkers had their clubs or enough put by, but the closed pubs and the open chapels had a depressing effect on the spirit.

'They'll be howling their horrible hymns,' she said, 'and flattering God, and telling him lies about himself. I bet he spends Sunday with the divine fingers bunged down the divine ears. I do myself.' She was restless. There was nothing to do on Sundays since the Pope went mad. 'It's because they've abandoned Christ,' she explained, 'and taken up with *Jesus*, soppy little Jesus Jones, meek and mild and gassing away gormlessly in the vernacular. They're so keen to keep up with the times, and down with the Joneses, and the lowest common denomination, they've forgotten all about eternity.'

'Oh, do shut up, Rose,' said Angela. 'I can't tell you how *boring* religion is. Do talk about something else.'

'It's this peculiar mix of iconoclasm and idolatry,' said Rose. 'They've put away the glorious vision and made this horrid, utilitarian, just-add-water creature in their own images. Some of them think he was a Protestant, some of them think he was a clown, some of them think he was a pouff, one of them thinks he was a mushroom,

180

some of them think he chased girls – and I think some of them think he *was* a girl.'

Angela kept her mouth firmly closed and gazed at the Sunday paper she held. Rose's contrariness was extraordinarily difficult to tolerate. Angela was certain that if the rest of the village had been on its knees Rose would have been going round denouncing superstition. 'If you want to talk about God,' she advised, 'go and see Teddy.'

'*Teddy?*' said Rose with contempt. '*Teddy?*'

Everyone avoided her – even Ermyn, who was soothed by the thought of a gentle motherly God and very weary of violence.

'*Stupid,*' said Rose, missing the twins, and bored and angry. She could hardly wait for the Day of Judgment. She would stand with her children on the mountain top, waving her black scarf.

* * *

On Monday morning there came a thank-you note from Lady Watcyn Hogge, and Gomer had not returned. Phyllis's face was very grey and set, as ominous as a winter sky pregnant with snow.

'She looks like yesterday's mashed potato,' said Rose. 'I'm getting fed up with her. She'd be impossible to replace. *Damn.*'

'She looks hungry,' said Ermyn oddly. And indeed although Phyllis had lost no weight overnight she had an undernourished appearance. Vengeance, said Ermyn to herself – she hungers and thirsts for vengeance.

'Cheer up,' said Henry to Rose. 'The twins will be home soon.'

Rose ignored the wry note in his voice. He was right. The morning seemed suddenly as fair as all the king's daughters.

'You should have a job, Rose,' said Angela astutely, over the breakfast table. 'You're supposed to have a brain.'

'What do you suggest?' asked Rose pleasantly. 'A few mornings a week at the gas showrooms, or a position in the Celtic Crafts shop?'

'You could go back and finish your degree,' said Angela.

'I don't want to,' said Rose.

And the twins lived at home, thought Ermyn. Rose's life was centred in the twins. They would never come home to a cold tea and a solitary, dusty bedroom.

'I must have been awfully drunk on Saturday night,' said Michael. 'I can't remember a thing about it.' He was looking at Ermyn, who stared back at him, self-possessed and indifferent.

'You were watching owls at one point,' she said. 'I nearly fell over you in the shrubbery.' She buttered a piece of toast in a noncommital fashion and ate it as though eating had become a mere duty and was no longer a matter for hunger or disgust or much consideration.

'I thought you were chasing sheep,' said Rose.

'Oh, we were,' said Ermyn. 'We did that too.'

Michael went red, and his eyes began to water. Phyllis watched him from the scullery.

He looks embarrassed, thought Ermyn. Perhaps he wasn't looking for owls. Perhaps he thinks I'm going to blackmail him. She took a dutiful sip of coffee and watched him over the rim of her cup, unblinkingly.

'You behaved beautifully, Michael my dear,' said

182

Angela. 'Not like that time at Jennifer's when you tried to drink whisky out of Charles's sandals. Have some toast, Edward.' She took a piece out of the rack and spread it with honey.

'Blodeuwedd,' said Ermyn.

'What?' they said, looking up.

'She was turned into an owl for being faithless.'

There was a clatter as Angela put her cup down, missing the saucer.

'What *are* you talking about?' asked Edward, rather pettishly for a guest.

'The woman made of flowers,' explained Ermyn. 'She was turned into an owl for infidelity.'

None of them had ever read the *Mabinogion*, any more than they'd ever read the Bible. They didn't know what she was talking about. She got up, pushed back her chair and left the kitchen without looking at them.

'Go back to bed,' called Angela. 'You still look pasty. Phyllis, has Gomer come back yet?'

'No,' said Phyllis.

Ermyn, outside in the passage, thought how silly they all were. She knew where Gomer was. It was obvious. He had thrown himself into Elys Water. What else could he do?

She walked down the passage as far as the hall, and then half-way back again. At the sound of Angela's voice she opened the dining-room door and hid herself inside. There were sweet, pink roses on the dresser and a blue-and-white bowl full of sugar lumps. Two petals fell from the roses with a soft sound on the dark wood. Outside the windows, the gardens lay as calmly beautiful as a gravid cat – she could nearly see the flanks of the lawn

183

moving. She wasn't surprised. The earth should heave in revolt at all the pain and tears and the blood and the dead it contained, at all the evil and the sorrow. It should go into reverse like death, become anti-matter. She swallowed hard. Her sort of person never gave way.

'The police,' Angela was saying to Henry in the hall. 'Phyllis is terribly worried.'

Ermyn watched them through the wide crack in the age-old oak of the dining-room door. She could see a pewter plate on the dresser gleaming with a dull Atlantic light.

'No,' said Henry. The Captain had never considered it any part of the duties of the police to concern themselves with the family's affairs, and Henry was, willy nilly, his father's son.

'But Phyllis is really upset,' said Angela.

'She's nuts,' said Rose blithely, passing by in her gardening gloves. She knew that Gomer would be up at the camping site by the lake. He had been there before doing odd jobs and picking up what he could in the way of girls.

'Just leave it,' said Henry. 'It'll be all right.'

*   *   *

Rose wandered the garden, cutting flowers regardless. When she came to the place where the path slipped into the lawn she stopped, looking at the pool of dried blood, diminishing into spots, with surprise and disapproval. 'Nasty,' she said. At once she raised her voice. 'Ermyn, *Ermyn . . .*'

'What on earth . . .?' called Angela from the terrace, looking up from her magazine – it was heavy and shiny

184

and its pages slid irritatingly together under her lightly oiled fingers.

'Nothing,' said Rose. '*Ermyn.*'

Ermyn emerged from the cool of the dining-room, seeming to walk with as much difficulty as a girl tied to a tree by a piece of strong elastic.

'Bring me a bucket of water and a broom, quickly and quietly,' said Rose.

But when Ermyn came back, Phyllis was behind her. She reared darkly above the lavender and sage, looked down and went away.

'She thinks it's Gomer's,' said Rose. 'She is now quite certain that Gomer was murdered on this spot.' She wondered whether to tell Phyllis where her grandson had gone and decided not to. Phyllis had been insufferable recently.

She scrubbed at the path. 'It *is* thicker than water.'

'Perhaps it is Gomer's,' said Angela. 'I'm sure we should tell the police.'

'It isn't arterial blood,' said Rose. 'I expect he had a nose bleed. It's the kind of horrible thing he would do.

Ermyn longed for rain. She knew that only the blood of the lamb could wash her clean, but she would have preferred rain. 'Who was it who tooketh away the sins of the world?' she asked Rose.

'The lamb of God,' said Rose, 'of course.'

'I thought so,' said Ermyn. Battle-shed blood looked more shameful than menstrual blood. 'It's paint,' she said. Blood was a secret – scarlet like all secrets. It should never be divulged.

'We don't know what happened on Saturday night,' said Angela. 'Some of those people were in a very wild mood.'

185

'They all left when the drink ran out,' said Rose, for the ears of Edward, who had joined them.

'Maybe that dog savaged the sheep,' he suggested.

'Oh Edward,' said Angela, leaning against him and laughing. Pauline's poodle was about the same weight as a grapefruit.

'There were some men in the lane,' said Ermyn tonelessly.

'Men?' cried Angela, laughing; but even she shivered a little in the kindly morning warmth. The word had suddenly seemed to hold such connotations of danger, of mindless savagery.

'Well, if we're not going to do anything, there's no point in standing here talking about it,' she said, smiling sensibly. 'Come along, Edward. The sun's heavenly on the terrace.'

'How she *can*,' said Ermyn, without interest, behind the retreating backs, and reflecting that Edward's hair was somehow reminiscent of the colour and texture of school dinner.

'He's attentive,' said Rose sagaciously. 'He listens to all that awful tripe she talks, and he puts her woolly round her shoulders if it turns cold, and he bent right down to stroke her foot when the silly cow dropped that wine bottle on it. He's clever, Edward. He's discovered he could have three heads, each more horrible than the last and still have his way with the ladies, just by remembering a few tricks. It's amazing how few men do know it. Most of them think romantic success is dependent on the dimensions of their willies – a view for which there is no evidence at all.'

Ermyn didn't care what they thought. The subject held

no charm for her. She had glimpsed Angela and Edward together in the shadow of the bushes on the lower lawn and wondered why eroticism had ever been considered a fit subject for art and what possible appeal it could have for anybody.

The path was clean. On the terrace Rose glanced at Angela's magazine. It lay open at an article entitled 'Whither the Orgasm – Singularity or Multiplicity?'

'Bit hot for porn?' she said.

'It isn't porn,' said Angela. 'Anyway, there's no harm in porn. It never harmed anybody.'

Rose went to arrange her flowers in the twins' room, humming. She wouldn't really have minded if a full-scale battle had been waged with maximum mortality in the lavender. The twins were coming home.

'Morning,' called the doctor, hurrying down the passage. 'Matter of time,' he said with terse professionalism and not unduly cast down. 'Morning, Amelia,' he called across the terrace as he reached the front door.

Rose took out the tray of coffee and a plate of *bara brith* that Phyllis had made for Gomer and hidden under a stilton dish in the china pantry. It was a thrifty peasant bread, invented to use up sour milk and left-over tea, with a handful of dried fruit thrown in to take the taste away, but Phyllis made tea specially and put in fresh cream and butter, and gave big slices to Gomer whenever he felt hungry.

'No point in letting this waste,' said Rose, eating a bit.

'My favourite,' said Michael. 'Good old Phyllis.'

'You,' said Angela coldly, 'can take Ursula's handbag back to her after lunch.'

'But it's *miles*,' said Michael.

'It may be,' said Angela. 'Her handbag must still go back, and you've got nothing else to do. You can keep an eye open for Gomer on the way.'

Michael glanced at her and put down his *bara brith*, as though one of the currants had revealed itself as a black beetle.

'Now, I wonder,' said Rose to herself, observing his sudden nervousness. There had been two glasses from the house in the pavilion. 'I think I must be stupid,' she said aloud, concernedly.

'*You*, Rose?' said Angela. '*You* stupid? Surely not.'

'Well, not really,' said Rose. 'I see now.' She did too. She looked at Michael with genuine, and therefore deeply insulting, amazement.

Ermyn got up and went into the house. She wished the twins were back. Rose was different when they were there – softer, kinder; and she seldom swore. The twins were a guarantee of safety: Rose would never put their milk-tooth confidence at hazard. Her bizarreness was greatly modified by the presence of the children. During her pregnancy she had not been for an instant any more uncanny than a gentle jersey cow . . .

'Well, I'll have to take one of the other cars,' said Michael off-handedly. 'I've asked Phyllis to have a look at mine. It's got a knock.'

*   *   *

After lunch Rose tidied the kitchen completely, and began to prepare the twins' supper. She had made a pink blancmange, of which anachronistic confection the twins were very fond. It was shaped like a cowering rabbit and

188

quivered oleaginously on a green wedgwood plate. She had put fresh raspberries in little glass bowls decorated with damask rose petals, and washed nasturtium leaves and wild sorrel to put in their salad. Now she began to make their stew. She cut a long slice from a shoulder of lamb and chopped it into neat little squares. These she put to brown in some green gold olive oil in a heavy pan. She quartered three green tomatoes and sliced three courgettes, and chopped up a bunch of green spring onions, adding a clove of garlic for its stomachic properties and its efficacy against evil. These she added to the oil and meat in the pan, together with a chopped green pepper. She stirred it once and put on the lid. Later she would drop in ten tiny new potatoes. Five each. Lastly she took some spinach leaves and a handful of watercress and minced them up finely, saving all the juice. At the last minute she would add this, and the whole thing would turn a marvellous faery green. With it she would serve bright buttered carrots. Sometimes she made them an episcopally gorgeous beetroot stew with rosy cubes of chicken and green peas, but green stew was their favourite.

'I'm off for the twins now, then,' said Jack the Liar from the kitchen door.

'Slowly down the pass,' said Rose, contriving to smell the air around his mouth. He seemed quite sober.

'Back about tea time,' he said.

Rose reminded the saint to watch carefully as the twins came over the pass.

She turned her head a little from the wind that sometimes came up from the sea even on the best days. She had brought the Noah's Ark down from the attic and told Angela she had found it at an auction when she was looking for antimacassars. It was obviously valuable and Angela was annoyed.

*   *   *

Ermyn leaned against the frame of the landing window waiting to see the twins come back and how Rose would greet them. She had no idea how long she'd been there, but her shoulder was stiff. She'd watched Jack drive into the lane and disappear between the hedgerows, followed by a cloud of blond dust. There was a blackbird sitting in the sycamore, pouring out great jugfuls of song, confident and untroubled. She watched it mistrustfully, her expression very like that of the visitors. It was a lying bird. She had seen it before, dead under the wall of the house, eyes closed to a thin grey rim, beak open and silent. There was something wrong with the world – something very wrong with that part of it contained within her own skin.

Michael's car stood in the yard shining expansively in the sun. Phyllis came round the side of the house and lifted the bonnet. How nice of her, thought Ermyn, to fix Michael's car when she obviously disliked him so much. The sun beat down on her wide flowered bottom. Without straightening up, she looked around, slowly and smoothly.

Ermyn watched. Phyllis's movements were not the deft, well-lighted movements of the nurse, but furtive and unkind, the movements of the assassin.

It made more sense, thought Ermyn. Phyllis didn't like Michael. She would mortally wound the car and in its death-throes it would destroy Michael. But Michael had already left. Ermyn had watched him go off in Henry's

190

car, carrying the alligator handbag. She supposed she should do something, but it would be so embarrassing and she was so tired. Besides, people got irritated when you interfered. Perhaps a more formidable, more executive girl would have marched purposefully out, questioned Phyllis, even scolded her – would have diverted her from her evil purpose. But not Ermyn. Not now. She would as soon have intervened in the course of a play. Let Cain pass by, she said to herself, for he belongs to God. She looked beyond the murderess and the sun-filled yard at the black Welsh cattle moving slowly over the fields that hung like an apron from the mountain's broad waist.

There was a faint sound from Father's room. Ermyn pushed herself upright and went across the passage, and opened the door to look in. Father was lying half in and half out of bed. 'Water, water, water,' he was shouting in a whisper, his mouth dry and dragged with pain, and then suddenly silent.

Ermyn closed the door. She knew no one called Walter. Her mother's name had been Celia. Downstairs the telephone rang. Ermyn went back to the window and put her shoulder against the frame. It was still warm.

'I was never born,' she explained silently to her surroundings. She wasn't prepared to move again, to leave the small warm moment. Outside was grief. She was astounded at the size and determination of the grief that awaited her – the enormous, sinewy, wild-beast strength of it. It was so infinitely more powerful than herself, so all-encompassing and so destructive. Outside, all over the world, the worst had happened, was still happening. 'Never be born,' she said to herself. 'I was never born.'

Henry walked into the yard and looked at the dashboard of Michael's car for the ignition key. Satisfied, he opened the door and got in.

That wasn't right, thought Ermyn; but she was too tired to say anything and there was still a scuff of dirt on the Chinese silk rug in the drawing-room. After a while she went heavily downstairs, wrapped in the previous moment that enveloped her like a caul. People born in a caul were magically protected . . .

Rose was putting the final touches to the twins' supper, buttering lace-thin brown bread – she wouldn't let the twins eat white bread – and unwrapping a tiny cheese from a cabbage leaf.

As Ermyn entered the kitchen from the passage, Phyllis came in from the yard. 'Michael taken the car, then?' she asked.

'No,' said Rose. 'Henry took it. Jack just rang from the top of the pass to say he's bringing Gomer back – he was at the camping site by the lake – but Jack's let the car boil again and it won't move, and Michael's got Henry's so Henry took Michael's and . . . Ermyn, why are you laughing? Phyllis, where are you going?'

But the silence was total, obdurate as the torturer, unheeding and dumb.

The kitchen was empty. Phyllis was running as fast and as futilely as the wind from the sea. Somewhere, in another world, someone was howling as the sin eaters of old must have howled, fleeing the houses of sorrow weighed down with strange sins. Up on the hills the wind swept softly around the old church where the saint slept on undisturbed.

Afterword

The Sin Eater was Alice Thomas Ellis's first novel. It was published in London in 1977 by Gerald Duckworth & Company, and the critics, for once, got it right – here was a stunning debut indeed. "One of the most original, funny and at the same time serious first novels I have read for years." "A brilliant first . . . Extravagantly good." "A joy to read." "A minor classic." "One of the most accurate portraits of contemporary British life which I have yet read." "A first novel of great interest, achievement and promise." It was short-listed for the *Guardian* Fiction Prize and won a Welsh Arts Council award as a "Book of Exceptional Merit."

My own awe-struck love for the book dates from eight or nine years after its publication. I had recently begun reading *The Spectator* – best-written magazine in English at the time – and had quickly fallen into the habit of opening each week's issue to the back pages where a trio of columnists chronicled events in their three very different stations of life. Looking down, as it were, I would find the "Low Life" column, Jeffrey Bernard's "suicide note in weekly installments." Looking up, "High Life," where Greek playboy Taki tattled on the jet-set. And then in between, right there on eye (and I) level, was "Home Life," Alice Thomas Ellis's concise, acerbic, and hilarious communiqués from the ever-uproarious domestic front. Of the three Lifers, Ellis was the one whose words I not only read but studied, trying to crack the secret of her prose's brilliant effects. The trademark Ellis sentence was honed and polished but bristlingly energetic, pared to essentials – never a word

193

wasted – but retaining musicality and humor. It was splendidly *brisk* writing, and gave an unusually attractive impatience to her narrative voice.

In the pages of *The Sin Eater*, which I'd eventually tracked down through a London shop that was helping me collect the books of the *Spectator* fraternity, I heard "Home Life" echoing in the sharp-tongued dialogue, the biting wit, the keen-eyed and economical delineation of a family's psychological and emotional in-fighting. But in the novel I unexpectedly found that the kitchen door of Ellis's social comedy opens on the timeless: in her fiction the here-and-now unfolds in the presence of the last things – death and judgment, heaven and hell. As Rose says during her final robust excoriation of the changes that in recent years have rendered the Catholic Church unrecognizable to her, "They've forgotten all about eternity"; in *The Sin Eater* I discovered that Alice Thomas Ellis's unique gift as a novelist is her ability to make us remember.

In this context it is interesting to note what the author herself had to say about how she came to write her first novel. "I was so annoyed," Ellis confessed, "that . . . I stirred out of my habitual indolence and wrote a book called *The Sin Eater*. I put it in the form of a novel, since novels give better scope for ungoverned rage than more sober works and I had to do something rather than sink into despair." This statement appears in *Serpent on the Rock: A Personal View of Christianity*, published in 1994, and the annoyance, rage, and encroaching despair to which Ellis refers stemmed from her Rose-like feelings about the current state of Christendom, and in particular the "whiff in the drains" she believed indicative of something seriously wrong with the Catholic Church. Addressed at length and in non-fiction form in *Serpent*, these abiding concerns of Ellis's are first voiced in *The Sin Eater*, where they are given a maliciously exuberant airing by Rose.

The last time I went to Mass — and it was the last time — there was the [parish priest] facing the congregation, standing behind his table and joining in the singing of the negro spirituals and the pop songs and Shall-we-gather-at-the-river. There has always been a hint of catering about the Mass, but previously the priest had the dignity of a master chef busying himself with his specialité. *Now he seems like a singing waiter in charge of an inadequate buffet. One is tempted to stroll up and ask for a double martini and enquire who on earth forgot to put the doings on the canapés.*

Rose's diatribes call to mind the vigorous "commination" which is said to have streamed in ancient times from the "contemptuous mouth" of the local saint, and it's this aspect of *The Sin Eater* that I would like in conclusion to call attention to. Ellis's striking use of Welsh legend and custom accounts in large part for the uncanny and disconcerting beauty of the novel. Think, in particular, of the immemorial figure with whose name the story is christened. The unusual ministrations of "the sin eaters of old" are referred to a number of times:

Rose affected to believe that Phyllis had made a pact with the Captain and would serve the funeral baked-meats from his chest, herself eating up the crumbs, together with all his sins, according to the old Welsh custom. . . .

Phyllis had put two glasses of British port on the coffin, handed them to Gomer and Jack, and watched while they drank it. Rose had been enthralled — could hardly wait for the service to end. "Did you see that?" she kept saying. "Did you see? The cwpan y meirw, *the cup of death. Some loony aborigines and the Welsh are the only people who ever did that, and the aborigines have stopped. Some of the them," she said, "thought they were ingesting the good qualities of the corpse and some that they were relieving it of its sins. The Welsh used to hire an untouchable to do it," she explained.*

Then in the novel's final paragraph, as a chilling howl of grief and fear shatters the air, it's as if the ancient untouchables – timeless as the last things – are again about their duties. In a book growing out of the author's anger at modern Catholicism, what are we to make of this? Perhaps that in the world of Alice Thomas Ellis's fiction, sin and evil and the need for redemption haunt the human heart beyond time. In this first novel, an old Welsh custom figures forth this unchanging truth. "Weighed down with strange sins," the sin eaters flee the houses of human sorrow, as they always have, as they always will.

*   *   *

The Akadine Press has previously published Alice Thomas Ellis's four *Home Life* volumes and *A Welsh Childhood*, her memoir of growing up in Wales. With this COMMON READER EDITION of *The Sin Eater* we begin publication of Ellis's fiction; over the next two years we will be bringing out COMMON READER EDITIONS of all eleven of her novels and her one volume of short stories. On behalf of all of us at The Akadine Press and A COMMON READER, I would like to thank the author and her agent, Robert Kirby of Peters Fraser & Dunlop, for making this project possible. I need hardly say how proud we are to be publishing the work of one of our finest contemporary writers.

Thomas Meagher
Editorial Director, A COMMON READER

About The Author

ALICE THOMAS ELLIS is one of England's most widely admired writers. Her fiction includes *The Sin Eater* (1977), which received a Welsh Arts Council Award for a "book of exceptional merit"; *The 27th Kingdom* (1982), which was nominated for a Booker Prize; and *The Inn at the Edge of the World* (1990), which won the 1991 Writers' Guild Award for Best Fiction. Her most recent novel is *Fairy Tale* (1996). Alice Thomas Ellis has five children and lives in London and Wales.